# DREAM MASTER
# ARABIAN NIGHTS

# Dream Master
# Arabian Nights

## Theresa Breslin

### Illustrated by David Wyatt

**DOUBLEDAY**

DREAM MASTER : ARABIAN NIGHTS
A DOUBLEDAY BOOK 0 385 604254

Published in Great Britain by Doubleday,
an imprint of Random House Children's Books

This edition published 2004

1 3 5 7 9 10 8 6 4 2

RANDOM HOUSE CHILDREN'S BOOKS
61–63 Uxbridge Road, London W5 5SA
A division of The Random House Group Ltd.

RANDOM HOUSE AUSTRALIA (PTY) LTD
20 Alfred Street, Milsons Point, Sydney,
New South Wales 2061, Australia

RANDOM HOUSE NEW ZEALAND LTD
18 Poland Road, Glenfield, Auckland 10, New Zealand

RANDOM HOUSE (PTY) LTD
Endulini, 5a Jubilee Road, Parktown 2193, South Africa

Typeset in Palatino by Falcon Oast Graphic Art Ltd.

THE RANDOM HOUSE GROUP Limited Reg. No. 954009
www.**kids**at**random**house.co.uk

A CIP catalogue record for this book is available from the British Library.

Printed in Great Britain by
Mackays of Chatham plc, Chatham, Kent

*for*
*Wendy and Jack*
*Storyteller Supreme and Master of the Dream*

'I control your dreams,
for I am a Dream Master.
My Dreamcloak releases
Imagination – and Imagination
is <u>the</u> most powerful force
known throughout all
Time and Space . . .'

# Chapter 1

'**Y**ou'll need to find somewhere *really* safe to hide your piece of dreamsilk.'

'Whaaat?' Cy glanced up from rummaging through the tall straw basket on his bedroom floor to look at the little man sitting cross-legged on his pillow. 'What did you say, Dream Master?'

'Your piece of dreamsilk.' Cy's Dream Master repeated irritably. 'The piece of dreamsilk that you tore from *my* dreamcloak. It needs to be kept safe.'

Cy pulled a pair of knee-length ladies' high-heeled boots from the bottom of the basket

and tossed them onto the assortment of things mounting up on his bed. Then he stuck his hand back in and pulled out an old dinner jacket of his dad's and a tambourine tied about with a red spotted scarf.

'Why are the contents of that basket more important than listening to me?' snapped the Dream Master.

'It's one of the storage baskets from our attic,' explained Cy. 'My friends and I are entering the big TALENT TV competition next Saturday and I need some props.'

'Talent!' snorted the Dream Master. 'Talent! I don't know what talent you think you possess, but it certainly isn't for listening!'

'Sorry.' Cy put down the Chinese fan and doll's enamel teapot he was now holding. 'Sorry, Dream Master. What were you saying?'

'I said that we need to hide your piece of dream-silk somewhere no one will discover it.'

'I put it away very carefully after our last adventure,' said Cy. 'Don't you think it's safe enough where it is?'

Cy's Dream Master shook his head and spoke in a firm voice. 'That's a piece of my precious dreamcloak you're talking about.' He pointed to the great cloak of dreams that hung down from his shoulders and spilled out across Cy's bed. 'A very *valuable* piece of my dreamcloak,' he said. 'And you've got it stuffed under that chest of drawers over there along with a whole load of other junk. In the wrong hands it could be extremely dangerous. Supposing somebody found it by mistake?'

'Nobody will find it,' said Cy confidently. 'Underneath the bottom drawer of my chest of drawers is a secret space that only I know about. And it's not junk that I keep in there, it's all of my private things. No one else has ever found that hiding place. Not Mum or Dad, not even Lauren.'

The Dream Master continued to shake his head.

'I'm very careful with things,' Cy insisted. 'Especially if it's got anything to do with the dreamcloak.'

'May I remind you that on the one occasion you were supposed to be looking after my dreamcloak you allowed your mother to put it in the washing machine!' the Dream Master said nastily.

'Oh, don't go on about that,' said Cy. 'I did say I was sorry.'

'I had to spend *aeons* in the fields of Elysium trying to recuperate from the trauma.'

'I got the dreamcloak back,' said Cy.

'Eventually.'

9

'And you did say that it's as good as new again,' Cy went on. 'Even the torn edge has mended itself.'

'I don't think you realize . . .' began the Dream Master.

Cy groaned. Why did adults frequently begin sentences with the words, '*I don't think you realize . . .*'

It was moments like this that Cy's brain switched off. He could feel it happening right now. His mind began to slide sideways and he couldn't stop it. Although, if he was being absolutely honest with himself, Cy would have to admit that his brain frequently drifted off somewhere else even when people weren't talking to him. At times like that, it wasn't that he was thinking of *nothing*, as his mum and dad or his teacher, Mrs Chalmers, often believed. It was just that he couldn't always remember on every occasion *specifically* what he had been thinking of when anybody asked him afterwards. It got him into the most amazing amount of trouble at school and at home. Cy's Grampa was practically the only person who didn't nag him about it. 'Your brain works like that because you are a free thinker,' Cy's Grampa once told Cy, 'like Leonardo da Vinci or Einstein. And, don't forget, they were the boys that changed the world.'

'Pay attention, Cy!' snapped the Dream Master. Cy blinked. 'Sorry.'

'Your small scrap of dreamsilk could be very dangerous,' the Dream Master said gravely. 'You tore it from my dreamcloak, remember?'

'Of course I remember,' said Cy. How could he forget? It had happened the first time he had ever met his Dream Master, when Cy had discovered that, with the help of his Dream Master and his dreamcloak, he was able to travel through Time and Space and dream his own dreams. They had been returning from the Valley of the Kings in Ancient Egypt and Cy had been gripping so tightly to the hem of the dreamcloak that part of it had ripped off in his hands.

The Dream Master gazed at Cy from beneath his bushy eyebrows and his eyes were serious. 'I worry about what might happen if that piece fell into the wrong hands. Dreamsilk has the potential to release Imagination. And Imagination is the most powerful force known through all Time and Space. Until you learn to use it properly,' he said, 'your piece of dreamsilk has got to be kept secure. Safe, Shielded, Screened, Sealed, Shrouded, Secret . . .'

'OK. OK.' Cy held up his hand. 'I get the picture.'

Cy went to his chest of drawers. He got down on his knees and pushed aside the stack of old comics that was piled up against the front. In the space underneath the bottom drawer, away from the prying eyes of his family, was where he kept his collection of favourite objects.

'The last time we examined your little piece of dreamsilk,' said the Dream Master, 'it had grown. It was getting bigger, becoming charged with your energy, *your* Imagination . . .'

Cy looked up from where he was kneeling on the floor. He realized that his Dream Master was trying to warn him about something. From previous experience Cy knew that it was wise to listen. 'And?' he asked.

'And . . .' the Dream Master spoke slowly, 'as you yourself have noticed, my dreamcloak has mended itself. The torn edge is sealed. That means that *your* piece of dreamsilk is now not connected in any way with me, or my dreamcloak. If you use your piece, if your Imagination is released through it, then it means that you may travel where I do not lead.'

'But I've done that before,' said Cy, remembering how once or twice, even without the Dream Master's help, he'd slipped into the dreamworld and managed to think his way out of dangerous situations.

The Dream Master raised an eyebrow. 'Efficiently? Competently?'

'Well, not exactly, I suppose,' said Cy.

The problem with running your own dreams, Cy found, was that no matter how hard he concentrated, something always went wrong. Being able to get inside his dreams, rather than having the dream inside his head like most other people did, could cause chaos in his life.

'Using your own dreamsilk also means that you can go where I cannot follow,' the Dream Master said gravely.

'I'd be completely on my own?'

'Utterly.'

Cy wondered how he would cope if he had to manage a whole dream by himself. He'd had one or two narrow escapes in the past when journeying through TimeSpace with his Dream Master – almost eaten by crocodiles . . . attacked by a mad Viking in medieval York . . . and driving a chariot through the streets of Pompeii as Vesuvius erupted around them.

'I think I might not be ready to do that,' he said.

'I *know* that you're not ready to do that,' replied the Dream Master. 'You must be properly prepared.'

'In what way?'

'Instructed. Tutored.'

'Oh, no!' said Cy. 'You mean like school?'

The Dream Master rolled his eyes. 'Possibly there will be slight differences.'

'No tests?' asked Cy.

'Only those of your own making.'

Cy pulled the bottom drawer of his chest of drawers out a little way and peered into the gap at the back. He could see some of the things he kept there: his fossil stone and the old Roman coin he picked up in Pompeii. Further behind these lay Grampa's war medal and the matchbox with the grains of sand from Arabia. Around and among these objects flowed the torn-off piece of the Dream Master's dreamcloak.

Cy tried to pull the drawer right out onto the floor, but he couldn't move it any further forward. 'The drawer's stuck,' he said.

'Let me have a go,' said the Dream Master.

'No offence,' said Cy, 'but if I can't open the drawer I don't see how you'll be able to.'

'Excuse *me*,' replied the Dream Master. 'I am the person who wrestled with Hercules, and *won*. Let me tell you, he'd have only managed about three and a half of his twelve tasks if I hadn't come along. And it was *I* who supported the immense

14

Giant Atlas as he held up the world, I who aided the Titans when—'

'I believe you,' Cy interrupted him. 'But it's not to do with strength. I think the reason it won't budge is because the dreamsilk is caught in it.'

'I have both strength *and* skill,' the Dream Master insisted. 'Who do you think helped Theseus find his way through the Maze of the Minotaur? That one couldn't find his lunch in his own lunchbox. He was dithering about for days until I came along. *And* I could easily have helped Alexander the Great unravel the knot of Gordian. But would he listen? No, he would not. A *very* impatient man. The history books don't tell you that.'

The Dream Master jumped down from Cy's bed, sweeping his dreamcloak behind him. 'Stand aside,' he ordered, 'and let me do it. You're not aware of my many talents because I don't show off, or boast, or tell tall tales,' he glared at Cy, 'like some people I could mention.'

'I don't tell tall tales,' Cy protested. 'I'm good at making up stories. That's different. My Grampa says I've got a wonderful imagination.'

'Too much Imagination can get you into bother,' replied the Dream Master testily.

'Actually,' said Cy, 'I've found that having an imagination can sometimes get me *out* of bother.'

The Dream Master paused. 'Indeed ... that is true. I recall the time when your storytelling skills helped you escape from some very angry Vikings.' A thoughtful expression came over his face. 'And there is another such person I met a long time ago, who told tall tales to save her very life ...' The Dream Master broke off.

From his position on the floor Cy peered up at his Dream Master. If he didn't already know how crabby, bossy and bad-tempered his Dream Master could be, then he would have sworn that was a soppy look on the little man's face. Cy bent forward and took firm hold of the handle of the bottom drawer to give it one last good pull.

'Who was that?' he asked.

'Mmmm?' said the Dream Master. His eyes refocused. 'Sorry ... my mind was slipping into another Time, what did you ask me?'

'Who were you talking about just then?' said Cy. 'Who was it who told tales to save their life?'

'*The* Teller of Tales.' The Dream Master sighed. '*The* Storyteller Supreme was a princess in fabulous fabled Ancient Arabia.'

'What was she called then, this Arabian princess?' asked Cy, now using his two hands on the handle of his chest of drawers.

'Shahr-Azad,' murmured the Dream Master.

'Shahr-Azad?' repeated Cy. Still hauling on the drawer he glanced over his shoulder. His Dream Master's face had again taken on a look of dreamy wonder. 'Who is *Shahr-Azad?*' he asked.

At that precise moment the drawer came unstuck. Cy rocketed backwards to collide with the Dream Master and land in a heap on the floor. There was a blinding flash of light and a dense cloud of purple smoke filled the air.

'You Butterfingered Buffoon!' shouted the Dream Master. 'You've gone and done it again! Dragged us into a dream without first thinking about it properly.'

'I don't think so.' Cy sat up, coughing through the swirling mist. 'We don't seem to have travelled anywhere. We're still in my bedroom, and nothing seems to have changed—' He broke off and stared at the space behind his bedroom door. 'Wh . . . Wh . . . What's that?'

'What? Where?' said the Dream Master, rubbing his eyes to clear them.

Cy pointed to the corner of his room where a lumpy-shaped roll of bright-red carpet lay on the floor. 'That wasn't there before,' he whispered. 'Where did it come from?'

The Dream Master gave Cy a fearful look. 'I don't know.'

Cy got up, took a step towards the strange-looking bundle, and reached out his hand.

'Don't touch it!' shrieked the Dream Master.

# Chapter 2

y stopped with his fingers only centimetres away from the roll of carpet.

'We might not be in a dream, and we might not have travelled through TimeSpace,' said the Dream Master, 'but there's a strange atmosphere in here. Can't you sense it?'

Cy closed his eyes and turned his head from side to side. He breathed in deeply. 'There's a strong perfumey smell, like spices.' He opened his eyes. 'But there's nothing else going on. No dreamweaving.' Cy's gaze came to rest once more on the rolled-up rug in the corner. 'And

that's only an old rug . . . I think,' he added.

'I don't like the look of it,' said the Dream Master. 'It looks . . . it looks as though it might be *alive*.'

'Sometimes you make such a fuss about things,' said Cy and reached out his hand again. But then he too hesitated. The carpet seemed to be vibrating softly with some unseen force.

'It's come from a different TimeSpace,' hissed the Dream Master. 'We have to find out where it came from and why it's here before you start meddling with it.'

'And how,' said Cy.

'How what?' said the Dream Master. 'I mean, what do you mean . . . "how"?'

'How did it get here?' said Cy. He glanced back at his chest of drawers. The bottom drawer was upended on his bedroom floor with the contents spilled round about. Cy crossed the room, kneeled down, and looked into the cavity underneath. All his precious things were still there, Grampa's war medal, the Roman coin, his fossil stone, the matchbox which contained the sand from Arabia. Cy's piece of dreamsilk was draped close to them, quivering gently.

'The dreamsilk is moving,' Cy whispered. 'I must have touched it as I pulled the drawer out.'

The Dream Master came and peered over Cy's

20

shoulder. 'You Gormless Great Galoot! You *know* that you have to be careful when you touch the dreamsilk. The dreamsilk controls the dream-world. Whatever you Imagine can actually happen. What were you thinking about at the time you pulled the drawer out?'

'Thinking?' said Cy. 'I was thinking . . . Um . . .' Cy felt again one of those awful moments of sliding despair that he got when he couldn't remember things that everyone expected him to. 'Um . . . I was thinking . . .'

'Well, *saying* then,' snapped the Dream Master. 'What were you *saying* as you pulled open the drawer?'

'Um . . .' Cy looked around vaguely. Then he caught sight of his matchbox which held the sand from Arabia. 'Arabia . . . That's it! We were both talking about Ancient Arabia . . .'

'Arabia . . .' The Dream Master glanced back nervously at the corner of Cy's room. 'Ancient Arabia.'

'What's so special about Ancient Arabia?' asked Cy.

'You've never heard of Ancient Arabia?' demanded the Dream Master.

'I might have read some stories from Arabia.'

'What is the matter with your school teachers

that you are not aware of important aspects of history?'

'We do *lots* of history,' said Cy. 'Vikings, and, and, Romans and Egyptians and Aztecs and Greeks and—'

'– And manage to miss out one of the most interesting. The cradle of civilization, where Magic, Myth and the Wonders of the World unite!'

'What's that got to do with this old rug?' said Cy, trying to stop his Dream Master ranting on and on.

'If it originated in Ancient Arabia,' the Dream Master spoke carefully, 'then that "old rug" might not be an "old rug". It might be a carpet – a flying carpet.'

'A flying carpet!' Cy exclaimed. 'Wow! A real flying carpet! Can we try it out?'

'Flying carpets do not fulfil all that they appear to promise,' said the Dream Master. 'I myself have not yet *quite* mastered the art of flying them precisely. There's always steering problems. Landing and take-off can be tricky. In the hands of inexperienced flyers collisions occur. Safety belts are not a feature, nor are individual passenger airbags.'

'A quick shot,' begged Cy. 'It would be *so* much fun.'

'Not if you fall off.'

Cy got to his feet. '*Please.*'

'Wait.' The Dream Master looked from the rug to the dreamsilk. 'It still doesn't explain why *it* came *here*. If you were touching the dreamsilk and talking of Arabia then we should have gone there, to Arabia.'

Cy bent and picked up his piece of dreamsilk. 'Look!' he said. 'The dreamsilk was covering the matchbox containing Arabian sand.'

'Even so . . . Why has it worked in reverse?' the Dream Master puzzled. 'Why did *we* not go *there*? Why did we not travel through TimeSpace into Ancient Arabia? What else happened as you touched the dreamsilk?'

'We were talking,' said Cy. 'You were telling me about a friend of yours, a storyteller?'

'Ah, yes,' said the Dream Master. 'I remember now. I was speaking of the most famed daughter of ancient Arabia, the great Teller of Tales herself.'

'That's right!' said Cy excitedly. 'I asked you who was the Arabian princess who told tall tales to save her life? And you said, "*The* Master Storyteller *was*—" . . .'

'Mightyful Magnificence!' the Dream Master interrupted. 'It cannot be!' A look of awe appeared on his face. 'Did we make contact with the Princess

23

without Peer? With the Great One herself?' He frowned in concentration. 'If it is true, then that would explain why your story was overpowered by another more powerful storyteller.'

All at once Cy recalled the name that he was struggling to remember. 'I know who you were talking about!' he cried out in excitement. 'It was a princess called Shahr-Azad!'

Then he stopped, and gripping the Dream Master's arm, Cy nodded at the dreamsilk in his hand. It had suddenly changed shape and now fluctuated and thrummed with life. At the same moment, from inside the carpet, in the far corner of Cy's room came a female voice.

'Who speaks my name?'

# Chapter 3

In front of the startled gaze of Cy and his Dream Master, the carpet in the corner of Cy's room slowly unrolled and out tumbled a young woman. She was wearing a white satin blouse under a black short sleeveless jacket, red baggy trousers and silver sequinned slippers.

'Omigosh!' said Cy. 'Omigollygosh!'

The girl rose to her feet and looked around her. 'Who called my name?' she repeated.

'Shahr-Azad?' Cy's voice came out in a squeak.

'Mighty Sultan, I salute you.' Shahr-Azad bent her head and made a graceful salaam in front of Cy.

'He's not a sultan,' said the Dream Master, rudely pushing Cy aside.

Shahr-Azad looked from the Dream Master to Cy and back again. 'But he was the one I heard call. He is the Sultan of my Story, Master of my Dream.'

'With respect, O great Princess,' the Dream Master bowed low before Shahr-Azad. 'With the *greatest* respect. This is no Dream Master. He is but a boy.'

'Yet it was he who spoke my name,' Shahr-Azad insisted. 'He is the Dream Master who summoned me.'

'He has no skilled mastery of dreams,' Cy's Dream Master protested. 'His dreamsilk is not yet a dreamcloak.'

The Dream Master pointed at Cy's dreamsilk. The square of material covering Cy's hand was the size of a very large handkerchief. 'It's a travesty of a cloak,' said the Dream Master, 'it's an apology of a cloak, it's an excuse for a cloak. It's, it's, it's not a proper cloak . . . like mine.'

Shahr-Azad gazed kindly at the Dream Master. She looked him over from heels to head. 'Small is beautiful.'

'Hurrumph.' The Dream Master cleared his throat. 'Princess, that is not the point. It is *I*, not he, who is a Dream Master.'

Shahr-Azad moved closer to the Dream Master and the smell of musk and oranges floated with her as she walked. As she passed, Cy noticed that her eyes were deepest violet. She gazed intently at the Dream Master.

'We have met before,' she murmured. 'I remember now. You helped me so much with my stories to begin with. You were the great Master of Suspense.'

The Dream Master made a gesture of dismissal with his hand

'It was nothing,' he said.

'And you are the boy's teacher,' Shahr-Azad went on, 'so he will learn how to use his dream-cloak well.'

'He doesn't have a *proper* dreamcloak,' said the Dream Master. 'Only a piece of mine which came off in his hand.'

Shahr-Azad touched the fragile softness of Cy's piece of dreamcloak. 'It may have been torn from yours but this piece is no longer part of your dreamcloak. It is his. He owns it. It owns him.' She turned to the Dream Master. 'You cannot hide his destiny from him, mighty Dream Lord that you are.'

'I did not intend to, great Princess. But he is not ready. He needs to be prepared.'

'You must teach him.'

'He is a very . . . challenging pupil.' The Dream Master gritted his teeth. 'His memory is erratic. For instance, it is likely that he cannot remember what he ate for dinner tonight.'

'I can *so* remember,' said Cy. 'It was . . . er, well . . . it was good anyway.'

'See what I mean?' The Dream Master appealed to Shahr-Azad.

Shahr-Azad smiled. 'I will help teach the boy.'

'You will?'

Cy noticed that the soppy look had appeared again on the face of his Dream Master.

'His ignorance is appalling.'

'Er,' said Cy, scrunching up his dreamsilk and shoving it into the pocket of his shirt. 'This isn't meant to be impolite, but I don't know who you are . . . exactly.'

'I am Shahr-Azad. Wife to King Shahriyar. Teller of many wondrous tales.' The Princess of Arabia bowed down before Cy. 'And you are?'

'Cy,' said Cy. 'I am Cy. Short for Cyrus. Cyrus Peters.' Cy returned Shahr-Azad's bow with one of his own.

Shahr-Azad went over to the tall straw storage basket that Cy had been searching through earlier. 'This reminds me of a story I once told about a gentleman called Ali-Baba . . .' She glanced at Cy, and he again felt the waft of her perfume. 'Would you like to hear it?'

'Yes,' said Cy.

'No,' said the Dream Master. He bowed and spoke apologetically. 'Best to save it for another Time, Princess. At the moment we must find a way to enable you to return to your own TimeSpace.'

'Perhaps,' said Shahr-Azad. 'First we should explain to this boy who I am, as he is curious to know . . .' she smiled, 'exactly.'

'Shahr-Azad,' said the Dream Master to Cy. 'Teller of Tales. Princess of far Arabia. Storyteller Superlative.' Suddenly he scowled and said crossly, 'It is an absolute indictment of your education system that you do not know who Shahr-Azad is. What are your teachers doing all day?'

'Tests,' said Cy.

'Tests?'

'Tests,' Cy repeated firmly. 'Tests. Tests. Tests. And more tests. The teachers prepare the tests. Then they prepare us to take the tests. Then we do the tests. Then the teachers mark the tests. Then the teachers have to write reports about the tests. By the time they've finished doing all that it's time for them to start the next lot of tests.'

'What about stories?' asked Shahr-Azad. 'When do you hear the stories?'

'Oh, we study stories,' said Cy.

'*Study* them!' exclaimed Shahr-Azad. 'Stories are for listening to, or reading. How does one *study* a story?'

'Everybody has to learn when to put a capital letter, and where a comma goes.'

'What has that got to do with the heart of a story?'

'Well . . .' Cy hesitated. 'Em . . . I suppose it's useful. And we do tasks to find out about the story. We compare and contrast different ones.'

'Compare and contrast?' Shahr-Azad raised an eyebrow. 'You mean unfavourably?'

'Well, like,' Cy stumbled. 'You know . . . criticize how the writer has used the language. Sometimes we don't even see the original piece to begin with. It's been changed. And we have to work on that extract. Words have been left out or altered—'

'What!' cried Shahr-Azad. 'How can you learn to love the story if it has been spoiled or reduced before you even see it? Why do you do this?'

'Well, then we suggest alternative words, like other adjectives . . .'

Shahr-Azad shook her head sadly.

'. . . and then we revise and extend,' Cy finished lamely.

'What is it that they actually want you to *do* to the stories?' asked Shahr-Azad.

'Dissect them,' said Cy.

'Dissect them?' Shahr-Azad said faintly. 'Dissect stories?' She gazed in horror at the Dream Master. 'This is indeed a land of barbarians that I have been brought to.'

The Dream Master nodded his head in agreement.

'We must never forget the value of a story,' said Shahr-Azad passionately. 'The ability of humans to empathize is unique. Within a story we place ourselves in the shoes, in the minds of someone else. A story takes you where you have never been. Here . . .' she placed her hand on her head, 'and here . . .' she placed her hand on her heart, 'to know a different situation, to feel the emotions of another. In this Time, do they not know the importance of a story?'

'I think they have forgotten,' said the Dream Master. 'Whereas you, illustrious Princess, never forgot their significance.' He made a deep bow to Shahr-Azad and turned to Cy. 'The Princess Shahr-Azad's husband, a certain King Shahriyar was married many times before meeting her. And he had a habit of dispensing with each new wife the morning after their wedding. He married a wife one day, and the next he beheaded her. He did this many times until the brave and noble Shahr-Azad offered herself as his wife to prevent him executing any more young girls. To capture his attention and stay alive, on the first night she begins a story, but does not complete it. The King delays her execution in order to hear the end of the story. The next night the Princess completes that story and begins another. The King is bewitched and must hear the end of this one too. So night by night, and day by day, Shahr-Azad tells her tales and weaves her spell.'

The Dream Master bowed once more and Shahr-Azad inclined her head. 'Her stories are the most pleasing, amusing, confusing, frightening and wise.'

'Does a magic carpet feature in any of them?' asked Cy.

Shahr-Azad's own eyes followed Cy's gaze to where the red rug lay in the corner of the room. 'Ah. You have never flown upon a magic carpet?'

Cy shook his head.

'Would you like to?'

Before Cy had the chance to reply there was a thunderous knocking on the door of his bedroom.

Then Cy heard his older sister Lauren's voice shouting from outside.

'What are you up to in there, Cyberboy? Open up and let me in!'

# Chapter 4

Cy hardly had time to bundle Shahr-Azad into his clothes cupboard before the bedroom door crashed open, pinning the Dream Master behind it.

Cy's older sister Lauren stood in the doorway. 'Mum says you've got the big storage basket from the attic in here.'

'Beat it!' cried Cy.

'What do want from it?' demanded Lauren.

'It's nothing to do with you,' said Cy. 'Get out of my room.'

'I need that basket,' said Lauren.

'I've not finished with it yet,' said Cy. 'My friends are coming over and I want to look through it first.'

'So are mine,' said Lauren. 'Baz, Cartwheel and I are forming a girl band to take part in the TALENT TV competition. There are lots of prizes to be won. Loads of CD tokens for the best performers in these heats. Fame and fortune for those who make it to the regional finals. Solid gold medals for the national winners! We're having a rehearsal this afternoon and I need to find some real funky gear.'

Cy shuddered at the thought of Lauren and her friends getting together in his house. Noisy, moody, unpredictable Lauren and her two friends, Baz and Cartwheel, were a major pain in his life. Cy often talked with his friends at school about the trouble they had with brothers and sisters, and older siblings in particular. Even Basra, who had six in his family and had a lot to put up with, agreed that Cy's sister Lauren was a particular problem.

'It's because Lauren's in her teenage years,' Cy's dad had once reassured him when Lauren had spent a full fifteen minutes screeching on at Cy for borrowing a pencil from her room without asking. 'It's a phase your sister is going through. It will pass. She'll grow out of it.' But Cy could tell by the look on his dad's face and the tone of his voice that he wasn't totally convinced about this himself.

'Scram!' Cy told Lauren again.

'Oh, I get it!' Lauren advanced into Cy's room. 'You're going to enter the TALENT TV competition too! Well, you and your amateur amigos had better find another place to practise whatever pathetic performance you're putting together. We don't want you lot getting in our way.'

'I'd *rather* be somewhere else if you and your horrible mates are going to be here,' said Cy. 'I'll give you the basket when I've finished with it.'

'I want it now,' said Lauren.

'I've already told you I'm not finished with it yet.'

'Right...' Lauren smiled a nasty smile. 'I suppose I could always borrow something of yours.'

'Get away from there!' Cy shouted as his sister moved towards the cupboard in his bedroom. He leaped across the room and stood in front of the cupboard door. 'Beat it!!!' he yelled at the top of his voice as Lauren reached past him and put her hand on the door handle.

'Oh, be quiet,' said Lauren. 'You'll have Mum and Dad up here and then both of us will be in trouble.'

'It's you that charged into my room uninvited,' said Cy. 'I got the basket first and I haven't finished looking through it yet.'

'OK,' said Lauren. 'You sort out what you want. I'll wait.' And she sat down on Cy's bed.

Cy's eyes flicked desperately from his bedroom door to his cupboard door to Lauren, who was now watching him closely.

'Here, take it,' he said, and he pushed the basket towards his sister with his foot. 'Go on. It's yours.'

'Not at all,' said Lauren pleasantly. 'Suddenly you're being very helpful and nice.' Her eyes narrowed. 'You want me out of your room. Why?'

'I *always* want you out of my room,' said Cy.

Lauren stared at her brother. 'There's an odd pong in here. Have you been experimenting with a chemistry set?'

'It's none of your business.'

'What are you up to in here, Cyberboy?'

'Nothing,' said Cy.

'Ah . . .' said Lauren. 'The famous "nothing" answer. Which means that you *are* up to mischief.' She looked round Cy's room. 'Have you got something hidden in here that you don't want anyone else to see.'

Cy pulled some clothes and other objects from

the top of the straw basket. 'There. I've chosen what I want. You have the rest.'

'Not at all,' Lauren said in a sugary sweet voice. 'I insist that you look through every single thing and select what you need.' She folded her arms and grinned wickedly. 'I'll wait patiently until you've done that.'

Cy picked up the basket and thrust it at his sister. 'Here! Take the whole thing, and beat it.'

'No, darling bruv—' Lauren began, when suddenly her mobile phone bleeped and the front doorbell rang simultaneously.

Lauren pulled her mobile from her pocket, checked her phone screen and stood up. 'That's Baz and Cartwheel at the front door.' She took the basket from Cy. 'Incidentally,' she added as she marched out of the room, 'there is no way that you lot are going to win the TALENT TV competition.'

Cy slammed the door behind his sister.

The Dream Master unpeeled himself from the wall where he had been flattened by the force of Lauren's entry into the room.

'Your sister—' he began.

'I know. I know,' said Cy.

'– and her friends,' the Dream Master continued, 'defy reason. Have I got this right? Baz and Cartwheel telephone to tell her they are at the front

38

door at the same moment as ringing the front doorbell?'

'Yup,' said Cy. 'Where were we?'

Cy and his Dream Master looked at each other.

'The Princess!' yelped Cy and leaped to open up his cupboard. Out stepped the Princess Shahr-Azad. Cy gulped. Over the top of her filmy blouse and short waistcoat Shahr-Azad had put on Cy's Frankenstein T-shirt.

'This I like,' she said, posing in front of the mirror on Cy's wall.

'Princess,' the Dream Master spoke gently to Shahr-Azad. 'We must now arrange for you to leave.'

'Mmmm . . .' said Shahr-Azad. 'This TALENT TV competition, the one that I overheard your sister speak of . . .' Shahr-Azad spoke slowly. 'What is it?'

'It's a special TV company that's touring the country searching for new talent. I suppose it's another Reality TV show. They're in our area this week and people go along and perform what they think they might be good at,' said Cy. 'Singing, dancing, juggling acts, anything you've a talent for.'

'Your sister, Lauren, said there was much prestige in winning it.'

39

'Yes,' said Cy. He picked up his piece of dream-silk. 'Now, I'll try to concentrate my thoughts and return you to your own TimeSpace.'

'Fame . . .' said Shahr-Azad.

'Which you do not need,' said the Dream Master.

'Money . . . Gold . . . Your sister . . . mentioned gold.'

'You are richer by far than any gold that you might find here,' said the Dream Master in a distinctly worried voice.

'That's as may be,' said Shahr-Azad, 'but I think I may wait and see this TALENT TV competition.'

'No,' said the Dream Master and Cy together.

'You must return to your own TimeSpace,' said the Dream Master.

Shahr-Azad gave them both a steely look.

'Beat. It,' she said.

# Chapter 5

'**N**o,' said the Dream Master. 'No. No. No. No. No. No. No.'

Shahr-Azad flapped her hand at him and turned her head away.

'Princess, please listen to me. I am concerned for your welfare.'

At that moment an ear-shattering roar of sound vibrated through the wall from Lauren's room.

*'Yah, yah. Yah, yah.*
*We are the girls who say . . . YES!*
*Yah, yah. Yah, yah.*

*We are the girls who say . . . GUESS!*
*Guess what?*
*Guess why?*
*Guess who?*
*Who . . . Oooo . . . Oooo . . . Oooo . . . Oooooooo!!!!!'*

The Dream Master winced. 'This place is dangerous.'

'But interesting,' said Shahr-Azad.

'Princess,' said the Dream Master, ' "interesting" is not always pleasant.'

Shahr-Azad laughed, a low gentle sound. 'You are advising *me* as to the meaning of words?'

The Dream Master bowed. 'I would not presume to. You are the Single One who knows the power that words command, their substance, their force, and their subtlety.'

'This is true,' murmured Shahr-Azad.

'Nevertheless,' the Dream Master continued, 'there are people here who, if they found you, might do you harm.'

'I,' replied Shahr-Azad, 'have fought off wicked genies, flame-spitting dragons, and the terrifying deadly roc.'

'What's a roc?' asked Cy.

Shahr-Azad turned her gaze upon him. Her eyes grew wide. She drew in her breath. 'A roc is an enormous powerful bird, with eyes that can see all things: the snake in the sand, and the ant on the anthill. With strength enough to carry off an elephant, it devours those it captures by ripping their flesh asunder.'

Her voice wrapped itself around Cy's mind and in his imagination he saw the mythical creature with its cruel claws and vicious tearing beak.

'Its great wings beat the air,' Shahr-Azad's voice trembled as she continued, 'as it searches for its prey. Ayeee!' she cried out. 'It spies its victim! It swoops . . . to snatch a child from its cradle, a man walking on the shore, a woman sitting by a window.' Shahr-Azad lowered her voice to a sibilant hiss. 'No one is safe,' she whispered fearfully. Then she gasped, covered her mouth with her hand, and stared in terror beyond Cy's shoulder.

Cy jumped and looked behind him. There was nothing there. When he turned back Shahr-Azad was smiling and had wandered over to browse through the books on his bookshelf.

Cy glanced at his Dream Master. 'I see what you mean about the storytelling.'

The Dream Master cleared his throat. 'In addition to your safety, O mighty Princess, there is the question of responsibility. Your very name,

*Shahr-Azad*, means "Saviour of the City". And, by telling your stories and preventing the King executing all the young girls in his kingdom, you will rightly earn your title. Therefore you must return.'

'I have done my duty,' Shahr-Azad replied sweetly. 'I have told the King his story for tonight. He is more than pleased with me.'

The Dream Master wrung his hands. 'You cannot remain here.'

'Oh but I can,' said Shahr-Azad. 'And I will.'

'Why would you want to stay here?' asked Cy, 'when you can fly a magic carpet in a fantastic place like Arabia?'

'I peeked through the cupboard door. I saw how your sister is dressed, how her hair is styled. I hear how she speaks, what she says she can do. I want to be like her.'

Cy's mouth fell open. 'You want to be like *Lauren*?'

There was another rattle of sound from the adjoining wall.

'Go, girls, go.
Girls. Go. Go.
Go . . . O. O. O. O. O . . . Ooooooooo!!!!!!!!!!!'

'She comes and goes as she wishes,' said Shahr-Azad. 'She makes music which,' she paused, 'although it may not be entirely pleasing to all ears, is her own to make.'

'But a princess of Ancient Arabia has much more than anyone like Lauren or me,' said Cy.

'I do not have these.' Shahr-Azad lifted one of Cy's comics from his floor and began to leaf through it. 'K-E-R-P-O-W,' she spelled out a word. 'What does that mean?'

'It doesn't mean anything, exactly,' said Cy. 'It's just . . . em, it shows that action has taken place.' He glanced over her shoulder at the comic strip she was reading. 'You can tell what is happening by the illustrations. In this scene one person has punched the other person.'

Shahr-Azad frowned in concentration. 'K-E-R-P-O-W,' she repeated softly to herself, 'is a punch. Like this.' She swung her fist through the air. '*Ker*-pow. Ker-*pow*. **Kerpow**!'

Cy took the comic from Shahr-Azad's fingers and said, 'We need to sort out what is happening here.'

Shahr-Azad ignored him and went and picked up one of the long high-heeled boots from Cy's bed. Her fingers played with the zip. 'This is an extremely useful device,' she said.

'You'll have to wait at least another five hundred

years before they get around to inventing it,' the Dream Master said irritably.

Cy could see that despite Shahr-Azad's charm, the Dream Master was beginning to lose patience with her. He recalled how awkward it had been when in one of their previous Dreamworld adventures he had brought Aten, the boy from Ancient Egypt, into the twenty-first century. And then in another, how much trouble the medieval Viking invaders had caused charging about the present-day city of York.

'You could always return here another Time,' said Cy, ignoring the Dream Master's hard stare, 'when the house is quieter. I really want you to, because I'd like to try out your magic carpet again. But today is inconvenient. It's Sunday afternoon, all my family are here, and I've got friends coming over.'

Shahr-Azad was now sitting on the edge of Cy's bed, struggling to pull on the leather boot. She shook her head.

'Princess,' the Dream Master began again in a more determined voice, when suddenly there was a sharp rap on Cy's bedroom.

'Go away, Lauren!' shouted Cy.

'Cy,' a voice called out. 'It's Dad. May I come in?'

46

# Chapter 6

Shahr-Azad looked from the Dream Master to Cy. She was still wearing one boot and one silver slipper.

'Omigosh,' said Cy. 'Omigollygosh!'

Cy yanked open the cupboard door and Shahr-Azad hobbled across the room and disappeared inside. The Dream Master flattened himself against the wall behind the bedroom door as Cy's dad walked into the room.

'Everything OK?' Cy's dad asked. 'You're hanging on to that cupboard door as though your life depended on it.'

'Fine, Dad, fine.' Cy tried to rest himself nonchalantly against the door of his bedroom cupboard while keeping a watchful eye that his bedroom door remained open. 'Everything's cool. No worries. Great. Terrific.'

'Phew!' Cy's dad sniffed the air. 'That's some strong aftershave you've got there, old son. Better to be a bit sparing with it, especially as you're not even shaving yet.'

'Have you never heard of perfume for men?' Cy asked, trying to sound indignant.

'Uh. Right. OK. Sorry, Cy, I didn't realize ... Er ...' He inspected Cy more closely. 'Should I have a talk with you about, er, things ...'

'Like what?' Cy stared at his dad in bewilderment.

'Er, like ... growing up. You know. Becoming a man. That sort of thing.'

'Good grief! No!' said Cy in horror. And as his dad still looked uncertain he added, 'You told me all those things years ago.'

'Oh, that's right,' Cy's dad said with relief. 'Well, anyway, I came to ask you a favour. As you can no doubt hear, Lauren and her team are rehearsing their act for this TALENT TV competition. So, for the sake of peace in the Peters household, could you stay out of their way and possibly use the garage to practise whatever show you and your mates are planning?' He surveyed the collection of things cascading from Cy's bed onto the floor. 'What *have* you and your friends decided to do anyway?'

'Vicky and Basra and Innis and I are preparing a variety show,' said Cy. 'I was thinking of doing a few magic tricks. Everyone is into magic in a big way at the moment.'

Cy's dad lifted the little enamel teapot. 'I used to be quite good at conjuring. I haven't shown you my old coin-coming-out-your-ear trick for absolutely ages.'

Cy set his face in a fixed smile. The old 'coin-coming-out-your-ear trick' was one his dad had been doing since Cy was very small. And, even when he was small, Cy could plainly see that his dad had the coin in his hand all the time. 'I remember,' he said politely.

'If you need any advice. If you want any tips about sleight of hand . . .' Cy's dad made a few passes with his palms across the top of the enamel teapot, 'then I'm your man. Anything at all, you can always ask me.'

'Thanks, Dad.'

'I hope you get through to the finals next Sunday at least,' Cy's dad went on. 'Just think, if you were the overall winner, the world would be queuing up outside for your autograph. People love new talent. You might become incredibly rich. Fame and fortune would be yours.' He laughed. 'When you become a millionaire, don't forget your old dad, will you?'

'Yes,' said Cy. 'I mean, no, I won't. Forget you, that is.'

Cy's dad picked up the pair of the boot that Shahr-Azad had put on. 'Oh my!' he exclaimed. 'I remember the first time your mother wore these boots. You know this style is fashionable again.'

'Yes, Dad,' said Cy.

'Most styles do come back, you know,' said Cy's dad. 'If you wait long enough.'

'Yes, Dad,' said Cy.

'You young ones think you are so modern, but we've seen it all already.'

'Yes, Dad,' said Cy.

'Where could the other one have got to?' Cy's dad began to search around among the clothes on Cy's bed.

Cy wondered what his dad would say if he told him that it was on the foot of an Arabian princess called Shahr-Azad, at present concealed in his bedroom cupboard.

'I hope it hasn't been thrown out. Oh, what's this?'

Cy's heart flipped over.

His dad held Princess Shahr-Azad's silver sequinned slipper in his hand.

'Search me,' said Cy. 'Must be another one of Mum's shoes. Dad,' he went on, quickly taking the slipper, 'I don't mind practising in the garage, but I need time to gather some things together before my friends arrive.'

'Right-ho. I'll leave you to it.' Cy's dad grinned at him. 'You might want to go easy when you're spraying on the male scent. It smells like the Arabian nights in here.'

Cy closed the door quietly after his father left and leaned against it. 'This is exhausting me,' he said to the Dream Master. 'We have to get Princess Shahr-Azad to her own TimeSpace before I'm worn to a frazzle.'

The Dream Master unfolded himself once more from the wall. He opened the cupboard door and ushered Shahr-Azad into the room.

'Now,' the Dream Master told her firmly, 'we will make arrangements for you to leave.'

'I'm not going anywhere,' said Shahr-Azad. 'I heard what Cy's father said. He said that the world would welcome a new talent. That people would queue for many days to speak to the winner. He too mentioned Fame and Fortune.'

Shahr-Azad folded her arms. 'I am staying right here. I intend to take part in the TALENT TV competition.'

# Chapter 7

'But, but, you can't,' said Cy. 'Why not?' said Shahr-Azad.

As Cy opened his mouth to reply he heard his name being called once more from outside his room.

'This house is beginning to resemble Piccadilly Circus!' Cy turned around and opened his bedroom door as the Dream Master and Shahr-Azad took cover.

'It's only me again,' said Cy's dad. 'Your friends have arrived and I've asked them to wait for you in the garage. Please don't gorge yourself on

sweets and crisps all afternoon,' he added. 'Your mum has gone out and I said I'd make tonight's dinner. If you don't eat it she'll think it's because of my cooking and not the fact that you've over-loaded with E numbers.'

'Tell them I'll be down in a minute, Dad, will you?' said Cy.

He closed the door and, going over to his bed, lifted Shahr-Azad's silver slipper and handed it to the Dream Master. 'Here, take this and give it to the Princess. I have to go and see my friends, otherwise they'll come up here looking for me. *Please* use your dreamcloak to return Shahr-Azad to her own Time before I get back. And,' he lowered his voice, so that from her hiding place in his cupboard Shahr-Azad could not hear him, 'don't let her take the magic carpet with her. I want to try it out tonight. We'll return it to her later.'

Vicky, Basra and Innis were already in the garage when Cy arrived carrying his bundle of things from the house.

'Yesterday the TALENT TV Company began to set up tents in the big field near the wood on the edge of town,' said Basra. 'It's right opposite my house. My brothers and I went over this morning to speak to them.'

54

'When does the site open so that we can go and sign up?' Cy asked him. 'We need to get a slot for Saturday because we've got school during the week.'

'They told us that they need at least two days to install the power cables,' said Basra. 'So probably tomorrow night.'

'They are holding performance trials from Tuesday onwards. I read that on one of the posters,' said Vicky.

'Lots and lots of prizes at every stage of the competition,' said Basra.

'And the finals for going through to the regional heats are next Sunday,' said Innis.

Vicky counted on her fingers. 'That means, including today, we've only got six days to practise our act.'

'We need to have thought up a name by then,' said Innis.

'How about "The Mad Magicians"?' suggested Vicky. 'That might be a good name for our group.'

'How about "Magical and Mysterious"?' said Basra.

'I don't like a name that's got the letter "M" twice,' said Cy. 'It reminds me of Eddie and Chloe.'

'What? The Mean Machines?' asked Basra, referring to the name that their two classmates,

Eddie and Chloe, were known by because they went about picking on people.

'I think of them as "The Gruesome Twosome",' joked Vicky.

Cy and Innis and Basra fell about laughing.

'Let's get on with it,' said Cy.

He showed his friends what he had plundered from his own house and they began to discuss ideas for their show. Vicky had been given a one-wheeled trick cycle for her last birthday and, although she wasn't very good yet, she promised to practise for several hours every day until Saturday. Innis had decided on juggling. He was an expert basketball player and reckoned he could keep a few soft juggling balls in the air for several minutes. Basra was going to concentrate on special effects to give the act some colour and excitement, using sparklers, creating lightning flashes and setting off smoke bombs. Also Basra's dad had a friend who could obtain a cannon that would shower confetti into the audience.

Cy held up his dad's old dinner jacket. 'I was thinking of trying some magic tricks,' he said.

There was a silence and his friends glanced at each other. Cy knew why. He was famous in school for being clumsy not skilful.

'Give it a go anyway,' said Basra. 'We'll rehearse

during break-times at school and we can see how it works out.'

'Yeah,' said Innis. 'We can always change things around.'

'I've already looked up a few magic sites on the Internet and borrowed books from the library,' said Cy. 'There's a really good trick with a balloon that seems easy to do, and I can hide things inside the sleeves of this dinner jacket.'

They cleared a space on the floor of the garage and rehearsed in turns for about an hour or so.

'If we are to be as good as the other kids from our school who are entering then we need *lots* more practice,' said Vicky after falling off her bike for the ninth time. 'But I've got to get home now.'

Basra checked his watch. 'I can only stay for another ten minutes or so.'

'And me,' said Innis. 'My parents do that "all members turn up for family dinner" on a Sunday evening.'

In Cy's house, too, family dinner on a Sunday night was a must. On weekdays everyone ate at odd times as both Cy's parents had full-time jobs with extra commitments. Cy's mum worked as a modern languages teacher in a school nearby, and frequently stayed after hours to catch up with paperwork, or had parents' evenings. Cy's dad was a computer software consultant who worked away from time to time, and Cy and Lauren both did after-school activities. So Cy's parents insisted that on one day of the week they all sat down and ate together 'As a Family'.

As soon as his dad served dinner Cy began to bolt his food. He was keen to go upstairs and make sure all traces of Shahr-Azad's presence were gone. He hoped that she hadn't taken his mum's pair of old boots to Ancient Arabia with her. It would be hard to explain their disappearance, especially as his dad had seen one boot lying on his bed earlier. Cy forked a heap of rice into his mouth and started to chew. His dad wasn't the best cook in the world, despite the many gifts of cookbooks Cy's mum gave him.

'I thought I'd try a new recipe today,' Cy's dad said. 'Taste good?'

Cy's mum, Lauren and Cy all nodded, although Cy noted that nobody actually said anything. Cy reached for some water to help wash his food down.

'I've missed out on what's been happening today,' Cy heard his mum say. 'I was taking Grampa to do his weekly shop. So, what kind of day did you two have?' Cy's mum beamed a bright smile at Cy and Lauren.

Cy kept on eating and didn't reply. Well, he had been told often in the past that it was rude to talk with your mouth full. Lauren lolled her head from side to side and crossed her eyes. 'Oh, Mother,' she sighed, 'you're not trying to instigate a,' she held her fingers up and made an inverted-commas sign in the air, ' "Happy Family Talking At The Table" scenario. Please know that *The Waltons* we're not.'

'Our children are rehearsing with their friends for the TALENT TV competition,' Cy's dad replied on their behalf. 'We heard some *lovely* singing from Lauren's room.'

'And what about you, Cy?' asked his mum. 'What are you and your friends doing for the talent competition?'

'It's a secret,' said Cy. 'I'm preparing things privately, and,' he glared at Lauren, 'no one had better go into my room and start nosing about.'

'I don't need to go into your grotty room again,' said Lauren. She gave Cy a superior smile. 'When I was in earlier to get the storage basket I had a good look around. Nothing escapes my eagle eyes. I know *exactly* what you were up to in there this afternoon, Cyberboy.'

# Chapter 8

y's stomach gripped in cramp and some rice lodged in his throat. He gulped and tried to swallow.

'Your childish attempts at concealment are futile,' Lauren said loftily. She addressed everyone at the table. 'When I was in Cy's room earlier there was a strange whiffy smell and I know why.'

'You do?' Cy squeaked. He held his breath so tightly that his chest creaked with the effort.

'You're making magic potions!' Lauren declared triumphantly.

Cy breathed out through his ears.

'Concocting secret spells that make strange smells. Hey! That rhymes!' Lauren giggled. 'I must have natural talent. I'm doing the lyrics for our song for the competition.'

'Well if that's an example, then don't bother entering,' said Cy. 'And another place you're not supposed to enter is my room.' He looked at his parents and deliberately used a whiney voice. 'What's a person supposed to do to get privacy in this house?'

'Lauren, if you go into Cy's room without waiting for him to open his door to you then I'll allow him free run of your room,' Cy's dad said severely. 'Cy's bedroom is his own place. Everybody in this house has to be respected as a person and we hold privacy as an absolute right. It's not as though it's something dangerous that Cy is doing, is it, Cy?'

Cy waggled his head from side to side in what he hoped his father would interpret as a negative, but hopefully also did not commit himself to a lie exactly. Anyway, Grampa always said, the truth of things depended on your point of view. Grampa was a big fan of Einstein and held that all things were relative. So flying a magic carpet couldn't be considered dangerous if you received proper instruction. And before he attempted to do it Cy intended to receive proper instruction.

'There's nowhere really private any more,' said Cy's mum. 'I read in the newspaper that some surveillance satellites can zoom in on an individual person walking in the street.'

'You see, Cyberboy?' said Lauren. 'We've got you covered.'

'The police say that there's nowhere you can hide anything that someone won't find it,' Cy's mum went on.

'What?' Cy stopped with a forkful of food on its way to his mouth.

'They say burglars know all the favourite hiding places that people use.'

'No!' said Cy.

'Yes,' said Cy's mum, 'under the edge of the carpet, behind the cistern in the toilet.'

Cy relaxed.

'I remember one of my hiding places,' said Cy's dad. 'When I was young I thought no one knew about the space under the bottom drawer of a chest of drawers.'

Cy sat right up in his chair.

'Oh, everybody knows about that place,' said Cy's mum.

'Nobody would be stupid enough to hide any-thing *there*,' said Lauren.

They all laughed. Cy smiled weakly. The Dream

Master had been right when he had told him to find a new hiding place for the piece of dream-cloak. Cy felt for the piece of dreamsilk in his top pocket. He patted the outside of his shirt and then took his hand away and glanced furtively around the room. Where could you hide something so that it would be safe? There was always the top of the curtains, or . . . Cy's gaze came to rest on a painting hanging on the wall.

'Of course,' said Cy's dad, 'there was a programme on the telly the other night about places where people hide things at home and how professional burglars know all these hiding places. Hidden in the freezer, behind the curtains or a picture hanging on a wall . . .'

Cy's stomach fell lower and lower as his dad rhymed off the list.

'Maybe it could be a double-bluff?' Cy suggested. 'Like, maybe thieves *know* that people know that they hide things there, so they don't look in those places . . .' His voice tailed off.

Cy's dad shook his head. 'Don't think so, son.' He ruffled Cy's hair. 'It would only take them a minute to check all those spots first. That's not where I would be hiding anything valuable.' He grinned. 'So you'll have to find a different place to plant whatever treasure you might have.'

'Dad,' said Cy. 'It's not treasure I've got. But I would like a safe place to keep our props for the competition.'

Cy's dad went to the row of hooks at the kitchen door and took down the garage key. 'Here, Cy. You can use the garage until after the talent competition. The weather is fine enough to keep the car outside at the moment.'

'And even if it wasn't,' said Cy's mum pointedly, 'the garage is so full of old junk that you couldn't put the car in it anyway.'

'It's not only my possessions that cause the clutter in there,' said Cy's dad. 'Everybody else in this family has abandoned stuff in there over the years.

'We need to sort out the storage in this house,' said Cy's mum. 'Speaking of which. Did either of you find anything useful for your act in the old Ali-Baba basket I took down from the loft?'

'Ali-Baba basket!' A spatter of rice shot out from Cy's mouth. 'Why are you calling it an "Ali-Baba" basket?'

'That's what those tall straw baskets used to be known as,' said Cy's mum. 'Your dad and I were given that one as a wedding present when we got married. I guess it's to do with the shape. It looks a bit like one of these tall baskets in the Arabian stories. Was there anything worthwhile in it for either of you?'

'I got some old jewellery and a couple of scarves,' said Lauren, 'and Baz and Cartwheel brought some things over so we're almost fixed up.'

'How about you?' Cy's mum asked him.

Cy shook his head. 'Lauren took the basket away before I had a chance to look through all of it.'

'Well I'll leave it outside your door tonight,' said Lauren. 'Though what use you could make of our parents' antique clothing beats me.'

'Less of the "antique",' Cy's dad protested. 'Your mother and I are not that old.'

Lauren rolled her eyes at the ceiling. 'Spare me,' she muttered.

'I saw those fantastic high-heeled boots you used to wear,' Cy's dad went on, glancing fondly at his wife. 'You looked terrific in those.'

'Oh, yes,' said Cy's mum. 'Remember when we went to that big folk music festival? You were such a good guitar-player, dear.'

'Folk music festival.' Lauren screwed up her face and mouthed the words silently at Cy. 'Luvellee. *Not.*'

'You know . . .' Cy's dad said slowly. 'This TALENT TV competition is an open-to-all event, isn't it.' He winked at Cy's mum. 'Maybe us "antiques" should get some trendy gear on and enter.'

Both Lauren's and Cy's jaws dropped simultaneously.

'Well,' said Cy's dad smugly. 'That made them pay attention, didn't it?'

Lauren found her voice first. 'You're not serious? Please tell me that you are not serious.'

'Why not?' asked Cy's mum.

'You're doing this deliberately to embarrass me, aren't you?'

'Don't be silly,' said Cy's dad. 'It crossed my mind when I saw that old boot on Cy's bed. We used to beat out a mean tune or two, your mother singing, me strumming a few chords on the old guitar.' He mimicked someone playing a guitar. 'There are some skills that you never lose.'

'I'd be humiliated in front of my friends,' Lauren said.

Usually Cy did not totally agree with Lauren's take on family situations, but he was with her on this one. Could there be anything worse than seeing your parents dress up and perform in public?'

'Cringe Factor Five,' said Lauren. 'Please excuse

me from the rest of this meal. There's a TV show I want to see.'

Cy recalled that he had left his bedroom earlier with the contents of his chest of drawers tumbled out showing the space below. As Lauren flounced into the living room to watch her television programme he gobbled up the rest of his food. Now that dinner was over he needed to get to his room, find his mum's boots, hide the dreamcloak, and check that the Princess Shahr-Azad had been safely returned to her own Time.

'It's school tomorrow, Cy,' his mum reminded him as he got up. 'You have to pack your bag and make sure your homework's done.'

Cy's dad reached for a magazine. But Cy's mum was there before him and had it in her hand before he had time to pick it up.

'Darling,' she said, 'would you like to clear the table and stack the dishwasher please?'

'Well, not really,' said Cy's dad. 'I was hoping for a wee look at the Sunday papers before starting the working week.'

'OK,' Cy's mum said sweetly. 'I'll do the clearing up . . .'

'Why, thank you dear,' said Cy's dad with a grateful, but slightly puzzled, look.

Oh-oh, thought Cy, danger, danger, you're

probably being outflanked here, Dad.

'. . . and you can do the ironing,' Cy's mum continued. 'In addition to the clean bed linen, tea towels and tablecloth, that will include all the shirts, blouses and other things that you and the children will wear over the next seven days.'

'Uh.' Cy's dad stood up and began to stack the dinner dishes.

Cy melted from the room, galloped upstairs . . .

. . . and stopped at the top.

A trail of dainty white footprints led out of the upstairs bathroom across the landing and into his bedroom. Cy wrenched open his bedroom door and stopped just inside. His room looked as if a hurricane had hit. All his books were tumbled from the bookcase and his chair overturned. Clothes, games and sports gear were mixed together on the floor. Among all of this Shahr-Azad sat serenely on her magic carpet, combing tangles from her hair. A very stressed Dream Master was pacing up and down the room.

'What is going on?' demanded Cy. 'Why have you not returned the Princess to her own TimeSpace?'

'There is a problem,' said the Dream Master.

# Chapter 9

y grabbed the chair from the front of his desk and jammed it under the door handle. 'What is the problem? Why is the Princess Shahr-Azad still here?' he asked the Dream Master. 'If it's because she won't leave without the magic carpet then that's OK, let her take it with her.' He glanced anxiously at his bedroom door. 'Quite soon my mum will appear with my clean ironing for the week. And she always wants to chat on a Sunday night. She likes to ask me how I'm getting on at school and if I'll need any help during the week.'

The Dream Master looked keenly at Cy. 'Are those two bullies, Eddie and Chloe, still giving you bother?'

'They give most people bother,' said Cy.

'I thought your school had an anti-bullying thingamajig?'

'The Head started a campaign called "Beat the Bullies". There's posters and leaflets giving advice about what to do if you get picked on or see anybody being bullied, and the teachers hold special sessions each week about personal guidance. It works . . . a lot of the time.'

'But not always?'

Cy shook his head. He supposed that part of the reason that Eddie and Chloe often picked on him was that he stood out for being clumsy, and slow to absorb information in class. But then he'd noticed that the Mean Machines also went for some of the children of asylum-seekers who had come into school. They seemed to target anybody who was a bit different or who wasn't good at defending themselves. Which made them cowards, as his Grampa said. And though Cy knew this was true, it didn't help if he was having a bad day at school. He was glad his Grampa still met him after school each day and walked home with him.

'Bullies are better avoided,' said the Dream Master. 'Best to be where they are not.'

'That's what my Grampa says,' said Cy. 'But trouble follows me around. I seem to spend most of my day trying to sort out some mess I've made. Although this time,' he pointed at Shahr-Azad, 'it was *your* job to look after the Princess.'

'I was doing my best,' said the Dream Master.

'Then why are there white footprints on the landing?' demanded Cy.

'That may be talcum powder,' the Dream Master said, avoiding meeting Cy's eyes.

'Talcum powder!' said Cy. 'Who was using talcum powder?'

'I was,' said Shahr-Azad. 'Your toilet is intriguing, but very unhygienic.'

'You went to the bathroom!'

'I had to.'

'Anyone might have seen you as you went from one room to the other!' Cy cried out.

'I opened the door. I listened,' said Shahr-Azad. 'I heard you all eating dinner and discussing important things. I took my opportunity, although I have to say that I found your toilet precarious to climb upon.'

'You *climbed* onto the toilet,' Cy began. Then

he stopped. 'I'd rather not go there,' he said.

'Indeed, I too found it difficult,' said Shahr-Azad. 'And your bathroom is inadequately furbished. There were so few toiletries to choose from.'

'Our bathroom has *tons* of toiletries,' said Cy. 'Well, Lauren and Mum do at any rate. Dad and I have only a single shelf for our things, but Mum's, and especially Lauren's, take up the other four shelves.'

'It was not enough for my requirements.'

'Not enough for *what* requirements?' Cy asked. 'Omigosh! You didn't take a bath?'

'I merely washed my hair.'

'What were you thinking of?' Cy almost shouted at the Dream Master. 'You let her wash her hair in the bathroom! It's not good enough!'

'I agree,' said Shahr-Azad. 'It was not very satisfactory. There was not the choice of unguents and oils I would have at home in my palace. No sandalwood oil, no attar of roses, but I made do as best I could.'

Cy took the chair from the door handle, darted out of his room and ran across the landing into the upstairs bathroom.

'Omigosh!'

A scene of complete devastation met his eyes.

The bathroom was strewn with wet towels, cotton wool, wash cloths and sponges. Empty bottles of shampoo, conditioner, bath oils and scent were upended everywhere. Dollops of shaving foam and hair gel clung to the mirror. Among it all Shahr-Azad's footprints tracked through the thick snow of talcum on the bathroom floor.

'Omigosh! Omigollygosh!' said Cy.

Downstairs he could hear the noise of the television programme Lauren was watching, and from further away his mum and dad having a conversation in the kitchen. He reckoned he had about twenty minutes or so to clear this lot up before anyone came upstairs. Cy scooped up handfuls of talcum powder and emptied them into the bath. Then he ran the water to wash them away. He took several fresh towels from the linen cupboard on the landing to wipe up Shahr-Azad's footprints and clean the mirror and the rest of the gloop sticking to the walls. He rammed these down into the bottom of the laundry bag which hung on the bathroom door. Then he gathered up all the empty bottles and jars, stuffing the largest into his trouser pocket and carrying the remainder into his own room.

There he found the Dream Master pacing up and down. Shahr-Azad had braided her long hair into several plaits in the same style as Lauren and was quietly reading one of Cy's comics. Cy dumped the empty bottles he was carrying onto his bed. He opened his mouth to say something when there was a gentle tap on his bedroom door.

'The cupboard? Once more?' enquired Shahr-Azad.

The Dream Master leaped into position behind the door.

Cy opened his room door. His mother stood on the landing. She was holding some of the wet towels that Cy had buried in the laundry basket.

'Cy . . .'

'What?' said Cy.

'Lauren's complaining that someone has used all her bubble bath and bath salts, *and* her special aromatherapy lavender powder, *and* her tea-tree oil, *and* her essence of jojoba plant shampoo and conditioner, *and* her body lotion, *and* her hair mousse, gel, wax, spritzer, curl-enhancer. You name it. It's been finished.' Cy's mum was trying not to laugh. 'Cy, did you use *all* of these to have a bath?'

'As *if*,' said Cy

'Mmmmm, I thought it didn't sound quite right. Although . . .' Cy's mum hesitated.

'What?' said Cy wearily.

'Well, your dad was saying that when he was in your room earlier he noticed you seemed to be wearing some very strong aftershave.'

'So?'

'Well, your dad was saying...' Cy's mum paused awkwardly and then went on, 'that maybe you felt that you needed aftershave even though you weren't shaving.'

'And?' Cy was anxious to return to his room and deal with the chaos there.

'Well ... your dad was saying ... that perhaps your hormones had started changing ... that you were ... well, that you might appreciate a little chat.'

'What about?' said Cy

'Em ... growing up.' Cy's mum smiled, and then said seriously. 'You can always speak to me you know. It doesn't have to be a man-to-man thing.' She leaned over and tried to give Cy a hug.

'Oh no! *Mu-um!*' Cy moved smartly sideways. 'No! Really. It's fine. No worries. It's OK. No probs.' He tried to stay calm and gave his mother what he hoped was a steady, unhormonal look.

She smiled at him encouragingly, but didn't go away.

Cy saw that he would have to say something else. His mother needed reassurance or an explanation. He recalled Lauren's remarks at dinner about magic potions. It was *so* juvenile and embarrassing but he could see no other way of deflecting her attention. 'I may have used some of the bottles and things in the bathroom. I was looking for ingredients to make potions for our magic act for the TALENT TV competition.'

'OK,' Cy's mum said easily. 'I'm going to prepare some lessons for tomorrow now. But remember I'm always around if you need to talk.'

'Yo. Great.'

Cy watched as his mum went off downstairs. Then he nipped into his room, shut the door behind him and slumped against it. He pointed to his cupboard and mimed to the Dream Master. 'She has *got* to go.'

# Chapter 10

'The problem is . . .' The Dream Master held up his dreamcloak. 'This will not suffice.'

Cy looked at the beautiful iridescent cloak which billowed away from the little man's shoulders sweeping down and outwards in a great curve of magical dreamsilk. Deep within the folds it sparked and thrummed with life.

'Your dreamcloak is not at all faded,' said Cy. 'It is full of energy at the moment. Why can't you transport Princess Shahr-Azad back to Ancient Arabia?'

The Dream Master beckoned Cy to come closer.

'The Princess Shahr-Azad is a very powerful storyteller,' he whispered. 'When I try to draw her into another world she merely laughs, and I find myself being drawn into one of *her* stories. In your absence she has, so far, summoned a winged horse, a phoenix, Sindbad the Sailor on two occasions, and an ox, a donkey and a farmer.'

Cy gulped and looked around his room. Now he knew why it looked even more chaotic than usual. 'This can't go on,' he whispered in reply. 'We must find a way to get her out of my room.' He gave the Dream Master a worried look. 'What can we do?'

'Now that I have had time to think about it,' said the Dream Master, 'it occurs to me, that, un-important as you are, it may be that because you and your piece of dreamsilk brought her here, then only *you* can take her back.'

'*Me!*'

'Hush!' The Dream Master glanced over his shoulder to where Shahr-Azad was now sitting quietly reading one of Cy's comics.

Cy took his piece of dreamsilk from his pocket. He studied it carefully. There was no longer a ragged edge on one side to show where it had been torn from his Dream Master's cloak. It was, as Shahr-Azad had said earlier, complete. Cy gazed at it, and then at the Dream Master. 'I am beginning to understand,' he said, 'but I don't know quite what to do.'

'That's why you need instruction. You must learn how to manage the power that you have been given. But for the moment you must do the best you can.'

'You think I will be able to take the Princess back to her own TimeSpace?' asked Cy.

'I am not sure. But you must at least try.'

From behind them came a soft laugh. 'And if I choose not to go?'

Cy turned to look at Shahr-Azad. The Princess had stood up and was putting on her slippers. 'I'm sorry,' said Cy, 'but I have to make you disappear from this room.'

'Making things vanish requires certain skills and is extremely difficult,' replied Shahr-Azad. 'However, making things appear . . .' she rotated her hands in the air, and then placed her palms loosely together to form a hollow space, '. . . is considerably easier.' She opened up her cupped hands.

'Wow!' Cy let his breath out between his teeth.

A tiny bird was nestling in Shahr-Azad's palms. 'How did you do that?'

Shahr-Azad smiled and blew on her fingers. Cy looked again. The bird was no longer there.

'You see what I mean?' the Dream Master said to Cy. 'When I was trying to persuade her to leave she threatened to produce an elephant. It was at that point that I gave in. I did not think that a creature that size could remain undetected by your family for long.'

Cy realized that he could not risk battling with Shahr-Azad while his family were about in the house. Perhaps if he waited until later? He tucked his dreamsilk into his pocket, and as he did so his fingers touched a metal object. He pulled it out and gazed at it. It took him a moment or two to remember that it was the garage key his dad had given him at dinner. If he could persuade the Princess to go out to the garage there was less chance of her being discovered. Cy thought through his plan. He must not let the Princess know that he wanted her in the garage in order to take her back to Arabia. He would have to pretend that he was prepared to let her remain in the twenty-first century for a little while. 'I may have an idea,' Cy spoke aloud. 'I think I know where Princess Shahr-Azad might stay without being found . . .'

A few moments later Cy silently opened his bed-room door and sneaked out onto the landing. The Ali-Baba storage basket was lying on its side

80

where Lauren had chucked it out of her room in the general direction of Cy's bedroom door. From Lauren's room Cy could hear the low rhythmic thump of Lauren's music playing. She must have her headphones on, so hopefully she would not be paying attention to any other noises in the house. Cy leaned over the stairwell to spy out what was happening downstairs. The door of the living room was ajar, but Cy could almost guarantee that his father was dozing in front of the TV. The door to the little downstairs study room was closed. His mother would be preparing work for her pupils.

Cy took hold of the Ali-Baba basket and, as quietly as he could, he bumped it down the stairs. Carrying her magic carpet, Shahr-Azad tiptoed behind him followed by the Dream Master. They crept along the hallway and into the kitchen. From the back door Cy scooted along the side of the house to the garage, and then beckoned the other two to follow. Once all three were inside the garage Cy locked the door.

'My apologies, Princess,' said the Dream Master as he surveyed the garage which was full of family toys and tools. 'It is not as the castles of Arabia.'

'Yet there are many things here that I would not find in the King's palace.' Shahr-Azad trailed her

81

hands over the family bikes, the sledge and the beach things.

Cy pulled out one of the old dust-sheets sometimes used to cover furniture when his parents were redecorating and pinned it up at the side window so that nobody could see inside. Then he switched on the light.

'Oh!' said Shahr-Azad. 'How did you make the light appear?'

'From a power source,' said Cy. 'It's kind of complicated to explain but you flick this switch here and the light comes on.'

'To make this happen one merely presses a button?' asked Shahr-Azad. She spoke to the Dream Master. 'This civilization presses buttons to achieve things. Be watchful,' she turned her gaze upon Cy, 'if things are so easily achieved with so little effort that you do not lose the power of your Imagination.'

Cy put his hand in the pocket of his shirt. 'Everyone says that I have a good imagination,' he said. 'My teacher, Mrs Chalmers, and especially my Grampa, so now I am going to use it.' He took out his piece of dreamsilk and held it up. 'I *will* return you to the TimeSpace of Ancient Arabia.'

Shahr-Azad smiled and raised her hand in protest.

Cy spoke firmly. 'You *must* go back.'

Shahr-Azad opened her eyes very wide. 'You would not like first to try out my magic carpet?'

Cy looked into Shahr-Azad's violet eyes. He saw her sweet and gentle expression. But Cy knew that not everyone who appeared attractive had your best interests in mind. His Grampa's face was old and lined, yet he was a good person. And it was the same with Grampa's friend, Mrs Turner, the lollipop lady, who watched out for Cy on his way to school in the mornings. Her house had been bombed during the last war and she had been caught under the rubble. It had taken the rescuers nine hours to get her out. She walked with a limp, and didn't have many teeth left, but she was very kind. Whereas Eddie and Chloe, the Mean Machines at school who liked to pick on people, appeared OK on the surface. When Cy looked at his class photograph he saw that his two classmates looked like everyone else in his class, smiling away quite happily. You wouldn't know by their appearance that they could be so horrible.

Now Cy felt himself tipping into Shahr-Azad's soft gaze. She had kindly suggested that he might like a ride on the magic carpet, and he would love to do that . . . but he knew that the Princess was a trickster. Cy blinked. 'No!' he said briskly. 'I must take you back to Arabia, even if you do not want to go.'

'How would *you* like it if I placed you where you did not want to go?' Shahr-Azad asked him. She flipped her hand over the top of Cy's head.

There was the snap of air and a flash of light in the garage and then ... darkness. From far away came the Princess's laughter. Then Cy heard his Dream Master speak. It was the first time Cy had ever heard such a curious tone in his Dream Master's voice. The little man was pleading with Shahr-Azad.

'Let him out, O mighty Princess. The boy could suffocate in there.'

'No he won't,' said Shahr-Azad. 'There are plenty of spaces in the straw.'

She had put him inside the Ali-Baba basket! He was head over heels among all the clothes and other odds and ends with the lid shut down upon his head. Cy peered out between the gaps. He could hear the Dream Master and Shahr-Azad having a conversation.

'Princess, this is not fair. You have greater skill than he will ever have.'

'Let us see if he is able to free himself,' said Shahr-Azad.

So, Cy thought, it was a test of some kind. He

pushed against the sides, but knew that he would not be able to break through, and the lid of the Ali-Baba basket was jammed down tightly so he could not escape that way. Cy tried to recall the story of Ali-Baba. There had been special words to say. A password that enabled Ali-Baba to enter and leave the treasure cave.

'Open Sesame!' Cy cried.

The basket toppled over. The lid came off, and Cy crawled out. He sat among the bottles and debris from the basket and the bathroom.

Shahr-Azad regarded him with raised eyebrows. 'You surprise me, little storyteller. I thought I had you bound fast in there. You have more Imagination than I thought.'

She started to raise her hand, but before she could Cy held up his dreamsilk. He decided that he was not going to waste any more time. He concentrated as hard as he could. He thought of Arabian palaces and of enchantments. Nothing happened.

Shahr-Azad laughed at him. 'You do not have the knowledge to take you to my land.'

Cy's thoughts faltered. The Princess was correct. He knew nothing of Ancient Arabia. How could he transport the Princess back, how could he direct the dreamsilk, when he himself did not know

where to go? Then his eye caught sight of something beyond the Princess's line of vision. *He* did
not know how to get to Ancient Arabia, but he had
spotted something that possibly could. Cy focused
his thoughts . . .

Behind Shahr-Azad the magic carpet lifted from
the floor of the garage. It floated forward, waver-
ing for a moment as it reached Shahr-Azad. Cy
saw the Dream Master's startled look.

'No, Cy!' shouted the Dream Master. 'I don't
think that is a good idea!'

Shahr-Azad whirled round when she heard the
Dream Master cry out. But she was not quick
enough . . . The carpet went past her and hovered
in front of Cy. Cy jumped up and clambered onto
it. Then he reached out, grabbed Shahr-Azad by
the arm and hauled her up beside him.

'Shades of Sindbad!' yelled the Dream Master.
He ran across the garage, took a flying leap and
he too was aboard. Cy waved his dreamsilk in the
air.

'Go!' he commanded. 'Take us to Ancient
Arabia!'

The magic carpet undulated as a stream of air
blew under it. Then it jerked violently. Shahr-Azad
screamed. Cy grasped a handful of the fringes and
held on. The carpet nose-dived, falling through

wind and water, spinning, whirling. A galaxy of light, speckled gold and silver, spun about their heads. Time corkscrewed, and Cy, Shahr-Azad and the Dream Master were sucked into the vortex.

# Chapter 11

The enormous river of Time swelled around them and the magic carpet, carrying Cy, his Dream Master, and the Princess Shahr-Azad, hurtled onto it and began to ride the torrent like some manic white-water river raft. Cy kneeled at the front, Shahr-Azad and the Dream Master clung on behind him. The carpet crested the first choppy waves, rolled, tipped, then righted itself. The next foaming rapid loomed up and the carpet spun crazily towards it.

Cy desperately tried to hold on to his thoughts. He *was* a Dream Master, he told himself, if only an

apprentice one. His features screwed up with the effort of directing his mind to lock into one single purpose. A fierce wind blew in his face while images, words, and ideas jumbled together in his head. His piece of dreamcloak spilled energy in a blazing trail of blue and violet meteor streaks. He was aware that Shahr-Azad was also trying to seize control of the carpet and make it return her to Cy's Time, and he felt the will of the Princess clash with his own. The magic carpet bucked and twisted as they both fought for mastery.

'If you don't stop this,' Cy cried out to her, 'we'll all go under!'

'*You* stop!' Shahr-Azad retorted angrily. 'Let me take charge and we will return to your TimeSpace.'

'We're going to Arabia,' Cy cried out. His voice was snatched and flung away in the noise of the howling wind.

'You wish to see the wonders of Ancient Arabia?' Shahr-Azad shouted. 'Then let me first show you its terrors!'

With a groaning crack a deep pit opened up and they plunged down into a chasm of Space. Great walls of craggy cliffs flashed past on either side as the floor of a valley rushed up to meet them. Cy heard Shahr-Azad mutter some words and suddenly before them a series of grotesque faces stared out with eyeless sockets, while sinewy scaly tentacles snatched at the carpet as it plummeted downwards.

'Brake! You Blundering Blockhead!' the Dream Master bawled in Cy's ear. 'Brake! Brake!'

Brake? Cy looked around wildly. Where *was* the brake on a magic carpet?

'*Think!!!!!*'

Cy thought. He held up his dreamsilk.

'Stop!' he ordered. '*Stop* . . . STOP!'

The magic carpet halted abruptly. Its passengers slid forward and teetered on the edge. The Dream Master was the first to recover. He wiped his face with his hands and then his hands on his beard. 'Thank goodness for—'

'Aaarkkk!'

From a cleft within the nearest cliff a huge bird rose from its nest and flew towards them.

'It's a roc!' yelled the Dream Master. 'They eat living flesh!'

The roc's malevolent yellow eyes had spotted them. It came swooping in, talons outstretched ready for the kill. The Dream Master ducked and Cy swiped at it as it swept past. It circled and flew at them again, this time descending with its vicious beak wide open to attack them as it came.

'It's a budgie,' Cy told himself. 'It's *my* dream,

*my* story, and I say it's a budgie.'

The roc faltered, its wings trembled, then found new strength as Cy's thoughts wavered and his mind lost the picture of the budgerigar.

'Aaarkkk! Aaarkkk!' The bird sensed its prey had weakened and it cawed in triumph as it returned, filling the sky above them with its immense shadow. Cy saw the terrible rending claws, its awful hooked beak . . .

'It's more like a parrot!' Cy cried, gripping his dreamsilk and sending a surge of energy through it with this thought.

There was crisp *pfutt*! The roc shrank in size, its plumage changed, and the yellow eyes took on a cheerful mischievous expression. 'Pretty Polly!' it squawked. 'Who's a good boy then?'

'Ha!' Cy relaxed.

Shahr-Azad hissed in anger and clapped her hands. The floor of the valley below them started to boil and seethe. The hissing increased three hundred-fold, and the rocks separated into thick strands, then coils, then a roiling mass of grey slitherings.

'Snakes!' Cy leaped up as one serpent raised its head above the level of the carpet to strike.

'String,' the Dream Master prompted him quietly.

'Sssss-string,' Cy stuttered in fear. 'I s-s-s-say it's ssstring.'

The snakes subsided and lay still.

Shahr-Azad's eyes glittered in fury. She spread her hands and made the motions of the waves.

The carpet now sailed over a calm sea. An old fisherman stood on some rocks preparing to cast his net. With a strong motion of his arms he threw the net into the ocean. When he drew it in, his net was full of stones and mud.

'The Princess is using her stories to confuse you.' The Dream Master spoke urgently to Cy. 'She is trying to draw us in. This is the tale of the fisherman who finds a strange bottle in his net.'

The fisherman gathered his net to throw it once more. He flung it high and wide, wide and high . . .

But this time Cy was ready. As the net unfolded to encompass them he guided the magic carpet to soar upwards and avoid it. He gripped the dream-silk more tightly and urged the carpet on. 'Not here,' he said. 'Go to the palace.' Cy repeated the phrase over and over. 'Go to the palace. Take us to the palace of the Princess.'

With a violent twanging sound the carpet whizzed out through a fissure in Time and Space and sailed into an evening sky crowded with stars.

Cy looked down. 'Omigosh!' he said. 'Omigollygosh.'

The day was losing its heat. The sun was low in the sky, its rays like flames of liquid gold bathing a dream landscape of woods and winding rivers, pretty mud-brick villages and cities with tall towers and elegant minarets. The magic carpet travelled on above these until it came to a magnificent palace whose windows were made of stained glass and whose walls were studded with many jewels. Thereupon the carpet floated down and settled in a marble courtyard where fountains splashed and doves cooed softly.

'Are we in Arabia?' Cy asked the Dream Master.

'We are indeed. Well done, Cy.'

The Princess dismounted first and immediately turned on Cy. 'You lowly dung beetle!' she screeched. 'The wrath of a princess is upon your head!'

Cy stared in amazement. Here was someone who could screech even louder than Lauren! 'Don't be a bad sport,' he said. Cy quoted his Grampa. 'Sometimes it's good to lose. Then you enjoy the times you win even more.'

The Princess smiled, showing all her teeth. 'I will very much enjoy the time I win, because that time is now. I have you in my power. I could easily have your head chopped off. You will wait here until I decide what to do with you.' She clicked her fingers. The magic carpet rolled itself up tightly. Shahr-Azad tucked it under one arm, spun on her heel and disappeared through one of the archways.

The Dream Master looked fearfully at Cy. 'Let me see your dreamsilk,' he said. And as Cy showed him the now greyish piece of material, he went on, 'I thought as much. You've drained all your energy by keeping us on track to arrive in Arabia. And because it's your dream, your story, I can't use my own dreamcloak to help us escape.' The Dream Master glanced around worriedly. 'We're stuck here for a while, and I can't say I liked the Princess's tone. She is in a bad mood. A very bad mood.'

Cy folded his faded piece of dreamsilk and put it away. He went over and trailed his fingers in the fountain. Around the courtyard grew trees laden with peaches and pears. 'This is a fabulous place,' he said. 'I don't mind staying on for a bit. I'd like to explore the palace.'

The Dream Master bit his beard. 'You Great Gallumphing Gullible Gowk! Do you think you're on some kind of holiday tour? We'd better find somewhere to hide before—'

He was interrupted by the sound of marching feet.

The Dream Master scuttled across the courtyard and took cover behind a pillar.

'What are you doing?' Cy asked him. 'What are you afraid of?'

'Get over here! Fast!' urged the Dream Master. 'That sounds like the Palace Guard and, believe me, they won't be bringing us an invitation to share some sherbet.'

Cy made a dash towards the Dream Master's hiding place, just as a group of fierce-looking soldiers strode into the courtyard.

'Perhaps if we explained to them that we are only visiting for a few hours . . .' Cy broke off.

The captain of the Palace Guard let out a mighty whoop and brandished his scimitar in the air. 'Invaders! They lurk behind the pillar yonder. A silver coin to the man who captures them, dead or alive!'

'You can stay and explain if you want to,' said the Dream Master. 'I'm out of here!'

# Chapter 12

Cy hadn't realized that the little man could run so incredibly fast.

'Wait for me!' he shouted, as he raced after the fleeing figure of his Dream Master down the long walkway under the arches and out into a walled garden.

'Get them!' bellowed the captain of the Guard. 'They must not escape!'

And it didn't look as though they were going to, the thought came into Cy's mind as his Dream Master skidded to a halt in the middle of the garden and Cy cannoned into him.

'Look where you're going, why don't you!' The Dream Master hopped about, holding first one foot and then the other.

'Where *are* we going?' Cy asked him. The long garden was hemmed in by a high wall covered in trailing blossoms. Many paths wound this way and that, under trees and through arches surmounted by vines or scented flowers. A white peacock strutted around, its tail spread like a fan behind it.

'Look for a way out,' said the Dream Master.

Cy and the Dream Master ran to the furthest end of the garden checking the walls on either side as they went. There was no door in any of the walls. They were trapped!

Cy glanced anxiously at the entrance. 'I can hear the soldiers coming this way.'

'Hide in here while we think of a plan.' The Dream Master dived for cover under a large bush. The white peacock moved swiftly out of their way as Cy hurried to follow him.

'We might be able to get over the wall,' said the Dream Master. He crawled to the part of the garden wall nearest them and, grabbing a handful of the creeping plant which grew there, he tried to haul himself up. The branches came away in his hand and he landed back on the ground with a thump. He glared at Cy. 'Instead of standing there like a Potted Palm, why don't you give me a leg up?'

'What happens to me after that?' Cy asked him. 'After I give you a leg up, how do *I* get out?'

'I'll sit on top of the wall and help you climb up. I promise,' the Dream Master added as he saw the doubtful expression on Cy's face. 'Come *on*. There's nothing else we can do.' His fingers tightened on Cy's arm and he nodded towards the entrance to the garden. 'Look!'

The soldiers of the Palace Guard had appeared and, after hesitating at first, began to move towards them, searching the garden as they came by prodding the undergrowth and delving into every bush with their sharp swords.

'You want to stay here and become part of a kebab?' the Dream Master enquired with false politeness.

'All right,' Cy reluctantly agreed. 'But let's crawl along to where we're hidden a bit by that tree and then try it.'

'We'll have to be nifty,' said the Dream Master. 'And fast.' He cast a worried glance in the direction of the nearest soldier and then said, 'Now!'

Cy got up and crouching low held out his two

hands together to make a step for the Dream Master. As soon as the Dream Master had put his foot in place, Cy launched the little man into the air with a mighty heave.

'Ayeeeeeeeeeeee!!'

The Dream Master had landed accurately, but painfully, astride the wall.

'There!' One of the soldiers sounded the alarm.

'Cut them down!' bellowed the captain.

The Dream Master leaned down from his position on the top of the wall and reached his hand out to Cy.

A scimitar slashed through the air as Cy scrambled to freedom. It missed him by centimetres. Cy leaped clear while just below him pieces of splintered rubble broke from the garden wall and spattered on to the earth.

They tumbled to the ground on the other side, the enraged cries of the guards echoing behind them. They both got to their feet, the Dream Master limping. 'I cannot run very far now,' he complained bitterly.

'You won't have to,' said Cy. 'Look. The market is opposite. We can mingle with the crowds and lose ourselves there.'

The market place was thronged with traders, shoppers and entertainers. Cy and his Dream

Master moved quickly past snake-charmers, and stalls laden with leatherwork, pottery, lamps, cloth, foodstuffs, spices, and a huge variety of fruit, bananas, dates, figs. Fires were being lit and people gathered round these gossiping, exchanging news and bartering for goods.

'The Palace Guard won't give up,' said the Dream Master. 'And even though this market place is huge we can't stay here for ever. We must look for a means to put some distance between ourselves and—'

He broke off. Cy followed his gaze to where a man sat with two camels tethered to large stones.

'Perhaps . . .'

The camel-trader spotted their interest. 'Two wonderful camels,' he declared at once, 'very cheap.'

'We don't have any money,' said Cy.

'Your shoes,' said the camel-trader pointing at Cy's feet. 'I will exchange these two camels for those shoes.'

Cy looked at his trainers. His mum would be furious.

'Give them to him,' ordered the Dream Master.

'One of those camels is totally decrepit,' Cy spoke to the Dream Master from behind his hand, 'and the other one looks a bit scary.'

The older camel of the two was kneeling

sleeping while the younger animal frisked about trying to bite through the tether rope.

'This one for the venerable gentleman,' said the camel-owner, enthusiastically kicking the old camel awake. 'Extremely peaceable animal. Only one previous careful owner. Little old lady who didn't travel far.'

The Dream Master surveyed the mangy camel. 'Can this camel actually walk?' he demanded.

'Of course. Of course. Very good camel.' The trader helped the Dream Master climb on. 'Now you, sir.' He reached out to snatch Cy's trainers from his hand, then had to shove Cy's camel roughly several times before it would lower itself onto the sand.

Cy stepped forward to mount it. The camel looked at Cy and then spat a long juicy squirt of spittle through its teeth and onto the sand at Cy's feet.

'I don't think this camel likes me,' said Cy.

'Whether the camel *likes* you or not is completely irrelevant,' snarled the Dream Master. 'Get on the blasted beast and ride out of here as fast as you can.'

Cy's camel rolled its eyes. Cy tried to ignore its murderous look and clambered into the saddle on the animal's back.

'Are the *effendi* quite settled?' the trader asked.

The Dream Master and Cy nodded.

'I'd hold on a bit more tightly,' the camel-owner told Cy as he cut the tether binding the camel to the huge boulder on the ground.

Cy's camel took off like a racehorse. The Dream Master's camel tottered a few steps and then collapsed, legs splayed out, in a heap on the sand.

'Please, nice camel. Get up,' coaxed the Dream Master.

Cy's camel began to run in circles. Cy realized that he wasn't actually going anywhere. The camel was trying to throw him to the ground. He looked back as he bounced around on his saddle. The Dream Master had lost patience and was yelling at the top of his voice.

'Move, you Lazy Legless Lump! You Dopey Dromedary! You Hopeless Humped Horse!'

A few people had gathered to enjoy the spectacle. They called words of encouragement to both Cy and the Dream Master. Across the tops of their heads Cy could see something else. Attracted by the noise the Palace Guard were shouldering their way through the crowds.

'Omigosh!' yelped Cy. 'Omigollygosh!'

He hauled on the reins. The camel stopped dead. Cy shot forward over the top of its head and landed on the desert sand. In moments he and the Dream Master were surrounded by soldiers.

'We're visitors,' gabbled Cy as they were dragged off towards the palace. 'Tourists really.'

'You trespassed in the palace,' said the captain. 'You stole two camels.'

'Stole?' said Cy.

'We didn't steal them,' said the Dream Master. 'We traded—'

Ignoring their protests the guards marched Cy and the Dream Master all the way to the palace. Once there, they were led down some stairs to an underground prison. Then they were thrown inside a cell and the heavy door clanged shut behind them.

'This isn't good,' said the Dream Master shaking head. 'Not good at all.'

Cy peered through the bars set into the prison door.

'When Shahr-Azad hears that we've been captured she'll rescue us . . . won't she?'

'It's totally dark outside, so by now the Princess will have begun to tell tonight's story,' replied the Dream Master. 'Once she has begun the King has decreed that no one must interrupt her. Her very life, and indeed that of others, depends upon it. Often her story lasts the whole night through.

Dawn will break before she can come to our aid. The Princess will be powerless to help us. The sun rising . . .' the Dream Master paused, 'the sun rising is the signal for events to take place.'

'What events?' Cy asked. 'What happens when the sun rises?'

The little man was chewing his beard. 'We will be brought before the King.'

'And then?'

'Then he will decide.'

'What?' Cy wondered why his Dream Master was not answering him directly. Usually the little man spoke right to the point. So much so in fact that he was frequently brusque and often rude. 'What will the King decide?' Cy asked him again.

The Dream Master ran his fingers through his beard. He looked away before answering. Then he said very quickly and all at once. 'To trespass in the palace is a crime punishable by death. Tomorrow morning the King will hold judgement and decide the time of our execution.'

# Chapter 13

'**E**xecution! You mean ... like ...' Cy's voice shook. He put his hand to his throat.

'Exactly.' The Dream Master thumped the cell door. Then he jumped up to try to see out of the window set high in the wall.

Cy stared hard at the cell door. 'Open Sesame,' he said.

'That won't work again,' said the Dream Master, 'you Dreaming Daftie. And anyway there are guards outside the door and windows.'

'Can't you help out?' asked Cy.

'It's *your* story,' said the Dream Master. 'It's got to be *your* ideas.' The Dream Master began to stride up and down. 'Have you nothing in your pockets that might be of use? A penknife for example? Don't all boys carry a device that takes stones out of horses shoes?'

'No,' said Cy. 'And even if I had, it wouldn't saw through these bars. They are too thick.' Cy felt in his trouser pocket. The only thing that had survived the trip on the magic carpet was one of the empty bottles from the bathroom. Although . . . Cy held the elegant glass bottle up to the light and shook it gently . . . it was not completely empty. There were a few grains of coloured bath salts still lying at the bottom. And the shape of the bottle seemed familiar. Cy remembered earlier seeing the fisherman casting his net by the sea. There had been a bottle trapped in the fishing net. 'The bottle . . .' Cy murmured. He turned to the Dream Master. 'When Shahr-Azad took the magic carpet close by the seashore, what was in the bottle that the fisherman caught in his net?'

'A djin,' said the Dream Master. 'What you would call a genie.' He looked at Cy and then at the bottle in Cy's hand. 'A genie,' he repeated slowly, 'but . . . believe me they can be more trouble than they're worth.'

'It's our best chance to get out of here,' said Cy. He pulled off the glass stopper and stuck it in his trouser pocket. Then he squinted down inside the bottle at the tiny residue of green and gold. With his free hand Cy touched the piece of dreamsilk in his top pocket. Drawing on the last of his dream energy he directed it towards the bottle as he spoke.

'Awake, O Genie, and do my bidding.'

For a few moments nothing happened. Then within the prison cell a breeze whispered. This faintest murmur of wind stirred the grains at the bottom of the bottle. Cy's fingers became warm as a dull heat started to beat within the glass, growing stronger, hotter. The grains swirled and merged, the colours blending into one another. Light danced, sparkled and the bottle shook violently. The grains melded to substance, the colours separating into distinct shapes. The green became a pair of trousers and the gold a pair of huge hooped earrings. A figure formed and expanded. With a crack of lightning and a heavy peal of thunder it poured out from the bottle, enlarging as it did so to fill the space in the air above their heads. The heavy hooded eyes blinked once and opened. Dark pools of red fire flashed from their depths.

Cy staggered and clutched at the Dream Master. 'It's a genie!'

A very petulant voice addressed them. 'Who has dared disturb the Djin of the bottle?'

Cy gaped. The Dream Master nudged him hard in the ribs. 'Speak up,' he said.

'Me.' Cy tilted his head to look up at the huge figure looming over him. 'Me. I did. That is, I summoned you from your bottle.'

'So . . .' The genie folded his arms. 'What is it *now*?'

'Sorry?'

'What do you want.' The genie made a tsking noise. 'I'm assuming you *want* something. Everyone *wants* something. Nobody calls me up to say "hello", or to ask how I'm getting along.'

'Well, yes I did want something,' said Cy.

'See? Knew it!' said the genie. 'No matter that I might be busy pursuing my own interests and would rather not be disturbed. As soon as *you* want something it's "Awake, O Genie, and do my bidding" and never mind that *I* might have other plans for the day. Well frankly I'm scunnered with this whole Genie-do-this, Genie-do-that, carry-on.'

'Scunnered?' said Cy.

'Scunnered,' repeated the genie, 'as in "fed up",

"cheesed off", "bored". *Give, give, give,* that's all I ever do.'

'Oh no!' said the Dream Master. He struck his forehead with his fist. 'This is typical! We get a genie with attitude.'

Cy looked up at the genie towering above him. 'But you're *supposed* to do what I want,' he said. 'You are a genie. I've heard about you. You're in films and things, and, and, a genie must do as the master commands.'

'Sez who?'

'It's traditional,' said Cy. 'It's the custom.'

'Yes, but do I have to put up with rudeness as well?' the genie demanded. With you lot it's "*I want, I want, I want*". Well, "*I want*" doesn't get. At the very least you could show a bit of civility.'

'May I have,' Cy began politely. 'That is to say, I'm very sorry to disturb you—'

'Get on with it!' the Dream Master interrupted rudely.

'I should like very much . . .' Cy began again. 'I realize that you are awfully busy, but I wondered if you would be able to . . . and I'd be awfully grateful if you would—'

'Spit it out!' yelled the Dream Master.

'– grant me a wish,' Cy finished.

The genie tossed his head. 'I'll consider it,' he said, but only if you say "please".'

'Please,' said Cy.

'Say "pretty please".'

The Dream Master growled into his beard.

'Pretty please,' said Cy. 'Pretty, pretty, pretty, please.'

'Oh all right,' said the genie. 'But that's one of your three wishes gone.'

'What?' said Cy.

The Dream Master flung his hands in the air. 'You Fuddling, Foolish, Fluffing, Footer—'

'Be quiet!' Cy shushed the Dream Master. 'What do you mean,' he asked the genie, 'that's one of my three wishes gone?'

'Regulations,' said the genie. There was a malevolent gleam in his eye. 'Whoever opens the bottle only gets three wishes and then that's it. Curtains. Finito. Otherwise I would be utterly fatigued, running here, going there, fetching and carrying. I mean, I've got to have some time to call my own.'

'Yes, but how can I have used up one of my wishes already?' asked Cy. 'I only asked if I could *have* a wish.'

'Well that in itself was a wish,' said the genie. 'Just because you didn't use the words "I wish" doesn't disguise the fact that it *was* a wish that you made.' The genie shook his head and the wall of the prison vibrated. 'Tough luck, kiddo,' he said to Cy. 'There are two ways to learn: the easy way and the hard way. One wish gone. Two to go. Get on with it. I don't have all day.'

'I don't think that's fair,' said Cy. 'You're taking advantage of me.'

'Stop bleating!' The Dream Master was now hopping from foot to foot with impatience. 'Make the wish to get us out of here!'

'Yes, but,' said Cy. 'I wish I understood how—'

With a scream the Dream Master leaped up and smacked his hand over Cy's mouth. 'Take care that you don't lose another wish!'

Cy shook him off. 'I'm only asking a question,' he said crossly.

'You were not!' The Dream Master snarled. 'Didn't you *listen* to what the genie said? You Incompetent Ignorant Idiot! Words are the tools of your Imagination, which is the most powerful force in the Universe. Be careful how you utilize them. They have the capacity for immense good *and* terrible destruction. At the moment, the way you are using your language means that you are actually expressing a desire for something. Check your thesaurus when you get back to school. If you get back to school,' he added darkly. 'There is some doubt in my mind that we will ever return to the twenty-first century. You don't seem to know how to wish for something useful.'

'I wish you'd put a sock in it!' snapped Cy. 'Put a sock in it and, and, vanish! That would be extremely useful. I would be able to get some peace to think and . . .' Cy's voice tailed off.

The genie gave a mocking laugh, and in the exact same instant the Dream Master disappeared. One minute the little man was there, berating Cy, the next minute there was empty space and a muffled echo of his voice. Cy's mouth opened and then closed like a goldfish.

'Well,' said the genie. 'Now you've painted yourself into a corner.' And as Cy's mouth dropped open again, the genie raised one finger. 'A word of advice. If you want your small-sized chum to reappear then you have to use your last wish to get him back. So think before you speak.'

Cy stared at the spot where the Dream Master had been. There was nothing there, not even a puff of dust.

The genie folded his arms triumphantly. 'I take it that your last wish is to return the quaint little fellow to your presence?'

Cy stared at the genie without answering. His

brain was beginning one of its awful slumps to the bottom of his head. This often happened in class or when someone, usually an adult, was asking him something really important.

'Whaaa-?' he said.

'Your third and final wish,' said the genie, 'will be to restore your diminutive companion. Quickly now. Make it and we're done.'

'I, I, I . . .' Cy hesitated.

'Come along,' urged the genie. 'You want him back, don't you?'

Cy opened his mouth once more to speak and then stopped. For once in his life he saw that being slow to reply might be an advantage. Why was the genie pushing him to agree to the third wish? If he made that final wish then the Dream Master would reappear, but they would still be trapped in the prison. At the moment, although lost, the Dream Master was safe. And . . . Cy thought carefully, if he used his last wish to get out of prison then he would be free and could then think of a way to find the Dream Master. Cy shook his head. He grasped the bottle firmly in one hand and spoke very distinctly.

'I wish to return to my own Time and Space immediately.'

The genie drew his eyebrows together. 'This is

not the way I planned it,' he said irritably. 'Are you sure?'

'Yes,' said Cy firmly, even more convinced that it was the right thing to do now that he knew the genie was unhappy about it.

The genie sighed. 'Such an amount of energy I have to use for this,' he said. 'And all for a scrap of a boy.' He folded his arms, and his eyes grew large in his face – great pools of smouldering flame, which spread deeper and wider until they lapped around Cy. The walls of the prison shuddered silently and then fell away, melting to reform in a different colour, a different material.

Cy pulled his gaze from that of the genie. He shut his eyes and rubbed them hard. When he reopened them he was in his own garage, the Ali-Baba basket tumbled on the floor, in the same position as he had left it before beginning his journey on the magic carpet.

'I—' Cy began.

'It's done and that's it.' The genie spoke very fast before Cy could continue. 'Three wishes. All gone. Bye-eeee!' And with a *floop!* he disappeared back inside the bottle.

Cy replaced the stopper in the bottle and sat down on the garage floor to think about his situation. He had managed to get rid of the troublesome Princess Shahr-Azad but was now also minus his Dream Master. Where could the little man be? Cy resolved that he would go into school early the next day and look up information in the library. He needed to know more about genies if he was ever going to recover the Dream Master. He was also a bit uneasy at the way he had left the Princess Shahr-Azad. She had been a very angry princess indeed. Something told him that their paths might cross again and he wanted to be more prepared for that meeting when it came.

Cy took the piece of dreamsilk from his top pocket. It was completely transparent. He decided that he was not putting it under his chest of drawers in his bedroom again, not now that his whole family knew that to be a good hiding place. He looked around the garage and caught sight of the little enamel teapot that had once been part of a doll's tea set. He put the piece of dreamsilk inside and flipped the lid shut. Then he reached up and placed the teapot and the little bottle containing the captured genie on the window-sill. As he did so his hand brushed against the old sheet which hung there covering the panes of glass. Cy adjusted the drapes so that no one would be able to see through the window and into the garage. But as he closed and locked the garage door the make-shift curtain moved a little in the breeze from outside. In his haste to pin the sheet up earlier Cy had not noticed that the garage window was unfastened.

# Chapter 14

n the school library the following morning Cy typed 'Arabia' into the library computer catalogue under the keyword menu. Then he scrolled down through the pages on the screen. There was a huge amount of literature about Arabia: non-fiction, travel, religion, history, geography, and many fiction books. Some of the stories Cy was already familiar with – the one about Ali-Baba, tales of genies, often known as djini, and the voyages of Sindbad the Sailor. If he had paid more attention to these, Cy thought, then he would have been better equipped to deal with

Shahr-Azad and the genie. Many of these stories featured clever tricksters. Cy couldn't find anything specifically on genies, but on a library shelf he found a book entitled *One Thousand and One Tales of the Arabian Nights*. He sat down at a table and began to read.

Now he knew why the Dream Master so admired and respected Shahr-Azad. She had been incredibly brave, offering to sacrifice her own life to save all the other women in the kingdom. Cy could understand why she wanted to stay a while in the twenty-first century. She must be bored and frightened, telling so many stories for so many nights, on and on and on, one after the other, never knowing whether she would live through the next day. Cy found an illustration of a giant roc. Cy shuddered as he recalled how close he had come to being eaten last night.

'Cy, do you realize the bell has gone for the first lesson?'

Cy looked up. It was his class teacher Mrs Chalmers. 'What are you reading?' she asked. And when Cy showed her she said, 'Oh. *The Arabian Nights*? That is a fascinating book. So many different types of story: twists in the tail, jokes, thrillers, romances. You know, if it hadn't been for the *Tales of the Arabian Nights*,' said Mrs Chalmers, 'then we would not have so many great stories today. They are the basis of many of our well-known plays and books.' Mrs Chalmers checked the book out of the library and gave it to Cy.

'Stories lead you where you cannot otherwise go,' Cy began absent-mindedly, then stopped suddenly. He realized he was repeating word for word something he had heard someone else say quite recently.

'Go on, Cy.' Mrs Chalmers was smiling at him.

'You place yourself in the shoes of the character and go with them to experience things from their point of view.'

'There is a saying from native North America,' said Mrs Chalmers, 'that you do not know another person until you walk one mile in their moccasins.' She looked at her watch. 'We're going to have to finish this discussion now and get on with some class work. We have a lot to get through this term.'

By the end of the school day Cy and his friends were completely exhausted.

'Do you think we should try to get a TALENT TV competition registration form tonight?' Cy asked the others as they left school together.

'I've got a violin lesson this evening,' said Basra. 'But if I've got time afterwards I'll go to the field and see if they are handing them out yet.'

'I'm going home to collapse,' said Innis. 'My fingers and shoulders are aching and my brain has gone kerplunk.'

Cy could sympathise with Innis. His own brain was a bit overstrained and it was good to hear that someone else felt the same.

'I want to spend some time practising riding my cycle on my own,' said Vicky. 'How are your magic tricks coming along, Cy?'

'My dad said we could use our garage all this week for rehearsing,' said Cy. 'I'm making up my props there, away from Lauren. I don't want her looking through my things. She's convinced that I'm brewing magic potions.' Cy laughed as he walked out the school gate with his friends.

Behind them, out of sight round the corner of the school wall, stood the Mean Machines. Eddie nudged Chloe. 'Did you hear that?' he asked her. 'They're using Cy's garage to keep their things for the TALENT TV competition.'

'I heard,' said Chloe. 'That might be worth investigating.'

As Cy walked through the school gate and crossed the road to meet his Grampa, who was chatting to the lollipop lady, he did not notice that the Mean Machines were watching him with scheming eyes.

# Chapter 15

'**W**e'll go to my house today, if that's OK,' Cy told his Grampa as they both said good-bye to Mrs Turner, the lollipop lady. 'Mum knows that's where we'll be. Me and my friends are going to enter the TALENT TV competition at the weekend and I want to practise in my garage at home. I'll need lots of rehearsals to get my own part of the act right.'

'What are you thinking of doing?'

'Basra and Innis and Vicky and I are putting together a variety show. And I'd really like to do some magic tricks for it, but when I mentioned

it to my friends they . . .' Cy's voice tailed off.

'What?' Cy's Grampa reached out with his hand and allowed his fingers to gently brush the top of Cy's head.

'Well, they didn't actually say anything out loud, but I know they think I'm too clumsy to be any good.'

Cy's Grampa looked down at him and held his gaze directly with Cy's own. 'Would *you* like to try doing magic?'

Cy nodded. 'I'd love to be able to perform a really neat trick. It would be so cool to make something appear and disappear.'

'Did your friends say that they didn't want you to do it?' Cy's Grampa asked him.

Cy shook his head. 'No.'

'Well then,' said Grampa. 'Give it a go and see how you get on. If it doesn't work out then it doesn't work out. But at least you'll have tried.' He smiled at Cy. 'You owe it to yourself to make the attempt. I told old Monty that a few times when he stopped by my tent in the desert during the war. Don't give up before you begin.'

An hour later in the garage Cy was almost ready to give up.

He had studied the magic books he had

borrowed from the public library and chosen the tricks that he thought he could perform best. One involved making an object appear and disappear inside a piece of cloth. Cy rummaged among the shelves in the garage until he found something suitable. It was an old-fashioned key. He tied one end of a length of elastic through the hole in the top and, using a safety pin, he secured the other end of the elastic inside the sleeve of his dad's old dinner jacket. He put the jacket on and adjusted the elastic so that the key hung just above his wrist. Then he pulled the key down into his hand and displayed it to his imaginary audience. He then pretended to wrap the key inside the red spotted scarf from the Ali-Baba basket, but did in fact loosen his grip on the key so that it shot right up his sleeve. He then opened up the scarf and the key seemed to have disappeared!

Well, that was how it was supposed to happen . . . Cy kicked the Ali-Baba basket gloomily. He'd been practising for ages, but no matter how often he tried, his fingers either caught on the elastic or his hands fumbled awkwardly with the scarf. He wasn't going to fool anybody with this one.

If only his Dream Master was here, Cy thought, then he would be able to get some input from him. Cy decided to check his piece of dreamsilk. Inside the teapot the small scrap of cloth lay as he had replaced it last night: unmoving, almost transparent. It would be days before there was enough energy to allow him to go searching for the little man. And anyway – Cy's heart lurched – where would he look? It came to Cy that he had not thought about the problem properly. Within the vast realms of Space and Time, where should he begin his search? Cy enjoyed reading history but knew that there was much more than he could ever possibly learn. His knowledge came from what he had been taught in school, some books of his own, and TV programmes he had watched. But there was more, much, much, more. And somewhere, among all of it, his Dream Master was trapped, or . . . Cy's head spun with a new idea . . . perhaps not . . . Maybe the little man was lost in the terrifying unknown, the place the Dream Master himself referred to as Uncharted Land . . . the Future.

Cy left the garage and went to the small room downstairs where the family computer was kept. He looked up 'Genie' on the Internet. Trawling through the main search engines didn't turn up anything that shed any light on how to find his Dream Master. There was loads of information about the stories from *The Arabian Nights* and the Princess Shahr-Azad, whose name was spelled several different ways, but nothing of any practical use to him.

That night in bed, Cy took his school library book from his rucksack and ran his eye down the contents page of the *Tales of the Arabian Nights*. He turned to the story about the old fisherman who found the bottle in his net. The fisherman had been lucky to escape with his life! This genie was not kind, or willing to grant favours.

After a while Cy put the book aside and settled down to sleep. His dreams, the ordinary run of the mill kind he had most nights, were particularly confused and chaotic. He was sailing the seven seas. Alone. Cy searched the whole ship but he could not find Sindbad the Sailor. Suddenly he was shipwrecked on a tiny island and the boat sank without trace. Then a massive earthquake disturbed the ground and revealed that the island was not an island after all. It was a huge whale. A killer whale! Its cavernous jaws opened. Cy saw the long tunnel of its throat and tried to swim desperately to safety. He awoke in the morning in a welter of bedcovers with a very sore head.

It was only when he was half way through school the following day that it struck Cy that nowhere in any of his dreams had he heard the voice of his Dream Master.

# Chapter 16

A t lunch-time in school that next day, Cy,
Vicky, Basra and Innis got together to
discuss their plans. Some of the staff had
volunteered to help pupils rehearse their acts in
the assembly hall. The noise was terrific. Violins
screeched, trumpets brayed, and the babble of
voices rose and fell as children recited poetry and
teachers gave instructions.

Eddie and Chloe had commandeered the
stage and were singing loudly and dancing about
together.

Basra had managed to get a registration form

for the competition. Cy sat with his friends while Innis, who had the neatest handwriting, filled it in.

'We need to decide on a name for our act,' said Basra.

'We could use the capital letters of all of our names,' said Innis. He scribbled on some scrap paper trying out different combinations.

'Bivc, Vicb, Civb,' Vicky read out.

'That's not working,' said Basra.

'I read an article in a magazine,' said Vicky, 'that to create a good stage name you should use names that have some meaning for you.'

'Like what?' asked Cy.

'They suggested the name of your pet combined with the name of your gran, or your favourite uncle.'

'For me, that's coming out as Tiddles Bob,' said Innis. 'I *don't* think so.'

'We had a hamster once,' said Vicky, 'but I've forgotten its name. What about you, Cy?'

'What?' Cy blinked. He had been miles away, thinking about his lost Dream Master. 'Sorry.'

'Everyone has to come up with at least five suggestions by tomorrow,' Basra declared as the bell for the end of the lunch break rang. 'Out of twenty suggestions we should be able to find one that will do.'

\* \* \*

Later that evening Cy asked his mum and dad if they had any ideas for a catchy name for the act.

'It has to be something that interests the audience,' said Cy's mum.

'Keep it short and simple, that's my advice,' said his dad. 'What name are you giving your group?' he asked Lauren.

'La Bazca,' said Lauren. 'But I'm not at liberty to reveal its origins.'

'I get it!' Cy said. 'It's the beginning letters of your names. Lauren, Baz and Cartwheel.'

Lauren glared at him.

'Well spotted, Cy!' said his dad.

'I think the name is of lesser importance,' said Lauren huffily. 'The key to getting attention is to have a really good gimmick.'

'From a business perspective I can agree with that. A clever promotional idea can help sell the product,' said Cy's dad.

'Like what?' asked Cy.

'Like vomit on stage,' said Lauren, flouncing out of the room.

Cy's mum took a tissue from the box on the coffee table and pressed it to her mouth. 'Hopefully there are other ways,' she murmured.

But Lauren was already on her way upstairs, singing defiantly:

*'Ay Ay Ay Ay*
*We are the girls who say No!*
*We are the girls who say Go!*
*Go On!*
*Go Out!*
*Go . . . o!*
*Oh! Oh! Oh! Oh! Ooooohhhhh!!!!!'*

Before he got ready for bed Cy went to the garage
and checked on the dreamsilk. As soon as he lifted
the lid of the enamel teapot he knew that there
had been a change. The piece of dreamsilk had
darkened, blue shadows moved among its folds
and a restless energy crackled along the edge.

Cy reached his fingers towards it and then
stopped. It was tempting to grab it in both hands
and let it take him wherever it might go. But he
mustn't. First he had to think, then make a plan
what to do. The force within the dreamsilk was
very compelling. His Dream Master had often
warned him about using it wisely. Cy knew that
dream energy was powerful – powerful *and*
unpredictable.

Cy decided he would wait. It was almost bed-
time now. It would be better if he used it here in the
garage tomorrow after school, when he was more
certain of not being disturbed. Leaving it one

more day would allow the energy to flood into all the corners, and it would also give him time to consider where to travel to within the dreamworld.

Before falling asleep Cy read another story from the *Tales from the Arabian Nights*. Everything he was finding out about genies only served to make him more anxious. All through the night Cy tossed and turned trying to think of what he might do once it was time to use the dreamsilk. He needed advice. He could see that now. Someone to talk things over with, someone who could help out. But whom could he trust to tell about the Dream Master? Who would believe him? Who would take the situation seriously enough to help him out?

It wasn't until he awoke the next morning that the answer came to him. As soon as he opened his eyes Cy sat up in bed with a start. There *was* somebody who could help him find the Dream Master.

Someone who had told the Dream Master that Cy needed instruction and help to learn how to negotiate through the dreamworld. The single person not likely to be outmanoeuvred by a crafty genie. One whose own wits would be more than a match for any sharp practice. For the simple reason that she too was an accomplished trickster.

The Princess Shahr-Azad.

# Chapter 17

It wasn't until late on Wednesday night that Cy got a chance to use his dreamsilk.

In the early part of the evening Vicky and Innis and Basra had come round and the four of them rehearsed their own individual pieces. Then they talked through how their show would actually run from start to finish.

'The competition rules say that each act is only allowed a maximum of four minutes,' said Cy.

'I've made a plan of how to put all the different bits together,' said Basra, who had been elected the master of ceremonies. 'And I've settled on our

name. I looked through everyone's suggestions and chosen "Magical Mixture". Sorry if the double M reminds anybody of the Mean Machines, but my dad said if we let certain people stop us calling our act the name we want then we'd be giving in to bullying.'

'I never thought of it like that,' said Cy. 'You're right, Basra.'

'It's a good name,' said Innis.

'Sums up what we're about,' said Vicky.

Basra had decided that the signal for the act to start would be him firing off the cannon straight up in the air so that some confetti scattered over the stage. This was to give the others time to assemble their props and get started. Vicky was to go first and cycle around on her own for a bit, while Basra lit his indoor sparklers. He had stuck rows of these along each side of the cannon. His idea was that they would ask for the stage lighting to be kept low and the little burning lights would create a magical and mysterious atmosphere. After setting off the sparklers Basra would refill the cannon with more confetti. While Basra was reloading the cannon, Innis would do some juggling, then move to one side to allow Cy to perform his magic tricks. During this part Vicky would keep cycling behind Cy. When Cy finished he would signal the end by bursting a balloon with a pin. At that moment Innis would stop juggling, Vicky would gracefully dismount from her monocycle, and Basra would fire the last load of confetti into the audience. This would be their finale and they would all take a bow together.

Basra had printed out his notes and gave everyone a copy. While they read through their parts he aimed the confetti gun at Vicky and showered her with coloured paper circles. 'Trial run,' he said.

Vicky laughed and shook the confetti out of her hair. 'I don't think we'll get anywhere near the final,' she said, 'but with a bit of luck we could win one of the prizes. There's more than five hundred CD tokens to be won.'

'We still need to practise lots more,' said Cy. He was now able to make the key appear and disappear from the red spotted scarf without too much fumbling, and was putting together a non-bursting balloon trick. This involved taping a small square of clear tape on each end of an inflated balloon, which meant that a long skewer could be passed through from end to end without the balloon bursting. Cy was covering the ends of the balloon with different coloured ribbon. At least this trick didn't involve him in any sleight of hand.

'Let's meet here again after school tomorrow,' said Basra, 'and have a complete run through, from beginning to end, of everything we're going to do.'

After his friends had left, Cy took the enamel teapot down from the window-sill. He opened the lid, and, lifting out the piece of dreamsilk, he laid it in his palm. With his other hand he opened the book of the *Tales of the Arabian Nights* and started to read the prologue aloud.

*'In the lands of Ancient Arabia there dwelt a mysterious Princess. Her name itself is a mystery, as, at various times, she has been known as Shahrayzad, Scheherazade, or Shahr-Azad . . .*

The dreamsilk in Cy's hand stirred.

*In any event, she was a courageous girl of noble birth . . .*

Cy's hand tightened around the little piece of cloth as it began to thrum with energy.

*. . . Shahr-Azad was both beautiful and intelligent, but blessed with one gift above all other . . .*

Moving within the folds of the material Cy saw faces, words, spinning planets, and the abyss of the unknown.

*. . . The Princess Shahr-Azad had the ability to tell wondrous stories . . .*

Hypnotised by the images in the dreamsilk, Cy's eyes left the book, drawn towards the shifting kaleidoscope of light and shadow.

*. . . Stories of such marvel and ingenuity that all who heard them were enchanted . . .*

The great portal of Time and Space yawned open. Cy wavered, closed his eyes and tumbled in. The book fell to the floor of the garage, its leaves turning over and over.

With a cry of fear Cy fell down through the Ages. Black torrents of Time rushed past him.

'Keep focused!' he yelled at himself. He must remember all the details he knew of Shahr-Azad so that he could reconnect with her again. It was important that he land inside the palace, but not inside the dungeon. Cy tried to remember something, anything, about the last time he had been in Ancient Arabia.

But now he had lost the book. It was left behind on the garage floor, wrenched from his grasp by the force of his entry into the dreamworld. Cy tried to slow down, but his thoughts, and the motion of TimeSpace, raced faster. Fantastical beasts reared out of the darkness. Hands tore at his clothes, and nowhere, nowhere at all was the guiding voice of his Dream Master.

'Help!' Cy cried out in terror. 'Help!'

Darkness rushed to meet him. The great maw of the unfathomable was overpowering him. He was completely lost, his mind numbed. At the end, as he lost consciousness, one name came to his lips.

'Shahr-Azad! Storyteller!' Cy cried out. 'Princess Shahr-Azad! Help me!'

# Chapter 18

The hands that came from the darkness had changed to tentacles, winding themselves around Cy's neck and arms, tightening as he tried to free himself. If only he could see more. Cy wrenched his face free and looked up. The silver slice of a crescent moon sailed in the sky above him. A sky so deeply blue, with stars in a pattern not familiar to him, that he knew at once he had landed in the Arabia of long ago. But where exactly?

Cy looked down at what was entwined around his body. It was the creeping foliage of a large

bush. He was in the walled garden inside the palace!

Carefully he disentangled himself from the branches that had wound themselves round him. He stood up. The garden was empty. Keeping to the cover of the wall Cy crept quietly along the length of the garden and out into the corridor that led to the courtyard. All was quiet. Directly opposite him were some stairs leading down. Cy could smell cooking – meat roasting with pungent spices and exotic herbs. That stairway must lead to the kitchens.

Flitting from pillar to pillar Cy made his way along the corridor in the direction of the courtyard.

'Cy!'

Cy stopped. Someone had called his name! His heart slammed hard against the wall of his chest. He could not take even one more step.

The voice was that of Shahr-Azad. How could she possibly know that he was here?

Then Cy heard another voice, of a deeper tone.

'Cy? An unusual name, my Princess.'

'An unusual individual, my King,' Cy heard Shahr-Azad reply. 'And very brave and bold, this boy named "Cy-Rus".'

Cy's breathing steadied once more. No one had seen him. He was overhearing a conversation taking place in the courtyard just ahead of him.

'Cy-Rus,' Shahr-Azad's voice became vibrant and enticing, 'was a clever and courageous young man who lived in a far off land.'

Cy gasped. The Princess was using him in her story! He remembered his teacher Mrs Chalmers once telling the class that storytellers and writers used fact to weave tales of fiction, borrowing scenes and characters from real life to construct character, setting and dialogue.

Very, very carefully Cy edged his face round the pillar. He could now see into the courtyard. In the centre, near the fountain, Shahr-Azad sat on her magic carpet. The King, a fiercesome-looking man with a long beard, reclined near to her on a great tasselled cushion. All around the courtyard torches set in brackets flickered, throwing grotesque shadows on the walls.

'In his Time he had to defeat those of ill-intent.' Shahr-Azad lowered her voice. 'But Cy-Rus was not without power. He was able to summon a necromancer, one of little stature but great cunning. The boy Cy-Rus had to wrestle with this magician to weave his own fate. But he was a young man full of clever tricks, and though the Dream Lord was mighty and wily, the boy was able to outwit him.'

He couldn't really object to the line this story was taking, Cy thought. Shahr-Azad was portraying him very positively.

'However, one day a great monster appeared . . .'

Cy looked around. He would have to find somewhere else to hide until Shahr-Azad had finished telling her story. If he remained here he might be seen by anyone passing along the corridor from the kitchen. Cy slipped quietly round until he was almost at the archway that Shahr-Azad had disappeared through on the first day he had landed in ancient Arabia. That way must lead to her rooms. He would try to find the right door and wait for her there.

Cy made to step forward and then drew back. Two large scowling guards stood holding spears, one on either side of the arch. He would never get past them.

From the courtyard Shahr-Azad continued with her story. 'This first dreadfully dangerous monster that Cy-Rus had to conquer was like a man, yet not a man.' Shahr-Azad raised the pitch of her voice and it trembled with fear. 'Behold!' she cried loudly. 'I will show you the likeness of the dreadful creature!'

Cy turned to look. In her hands the Princess held Cy's Frankenstein T-shirt! Close beside him Cy heard feet shuffle in the corridor. He shrank into the shadows. The two guards by the doorway had moved forward to be nearer to the courtyard.

Shahr-Azad held aloft Cy's T-shirt.

'Shudder, as I did, at the hideous face of the beast!'

As the guards craned closer to get a better look Cy slipped behind them and into the palace. Shahr-Azad's story sounded interesting and he would have preferred to wait to hear the end of it, but he mustn't forget why he had come to this Time.

He was in a little room. A thick curtain hung on one wall. Apart from that it was completely empty. Cy ducked behind the curtain and stepped through into another smaller courtyard. Here the air was heavy with the smell of perfume. Tall fronds of palms brushed a canopy which was draped above a bathing pool. Dozens and dozens of lamps lit the scene, some floating in the water, others placed on the beautiful ornate tiles which bordered the pool. Round the pool, set out on tables, were circular brass trays of dusted sweetmeats, fruits in heavy syrup, honeyed cakes. Thick towels lay in piles ready to be used. It was almost as if someone was about to take a bath . . .

The thought was hardly in Cy's head when, from the inner part of the palace, he heard giggling and the slap, slap, slap of many sandalled feet. Talking and laughing a troupe of girls came into the courtyard.

'Omigosh!' said Cy.

The first one who caught sight of him let out a small scream and clutched at the girl beside her. Then they all began to chatter furiously waving their hands in the air.

'Omigollygosh!' said Cy. He stumbled as he turned to go.

An older girl pushed her way to the front of the group. 'Who are you?' she demanded. 'You have no right to be in the ladies' quarters. What is your business here?'

'I am here to see the Princess Shahr-Azad,' Cy managed to gasp. 'I mean no harm.'

The rest of the girls crowded behind her pointing and squealing.

'What an odd colour his face is!'

'His hair is so peculiar!'

'Do you see his strange clothes!'

'Look at his round eyes!'

As they came towards him staring curiously Cy backed rapidly away. He tripped and fell, up-ending one of the little tables. The circular bronze tray went flying and the dishes of cakes and fruits cascaded to the ground.

Then the girls all rushed upon him at once. Cy raised his arm to protect himself, but he was not fast enough. The older girl had crept up behind him, lifted one of the bronzed trays, and now brought it crashing down upon his head.

# Chapter 19

**W**hen Cy opened his eyes he was lying on a long couch with his head resting on the rolled up magic carpet. He scrambled to his feet. The room he was in looked out to the main courtyard. Cy could hear the pigeons cooing from round the fountain. Behind him the door opened. He spun round. It was the Princess Shahr-Azad.

'Your head will be very sore,' she said. 'Being struck on the head with a large tray is not a pleasant experience.'

Cy put his hand to his head. It *was* sore and there was a large bump rising under his hair.

'You were lucky,' said Shahr-Azad, 'that it was the ladies of the palace who found you and not the Palace Guard. They are very loyal to me and smuggled you here without anyone seeing.' She handed Cy a little cup containing mint tea. 'Drink this. It will make you feel better. Then tell me why, after making your escape from our deepest dungeon, you decided to return.' She looked at Cy keenly. 'Alone.'

'I've lost the Dream Master.'

'You cannot *lose* a Dream Master,' said Shahr-Azad.

'Not *lose*, exactly,' said Cy. 'You see, in order to get out of the cell where we were imprisoned I Imagined a genie—'

'You summoned a genie – a djin!' Shahr-Azad stepped back and glanced around cautiously. 'Where is this genie?'

'Safely in his bottle,' said Cy, 'on the window shelf of my garage.' Cy saw Shahr-Azad relax.

'Genies require *very* careful handling,' she said.

'I know that now,' said Cy. 'This genie tricked me into disappearing my Dream Master.' Cy's voice trembled. 'I don't even know where to begin to find him.'

'So you thought you would begin where you last

145

saw him,' said Shahr-Azad. 'It was very brave of you to visit me again. Did you not think that I might still punish you for bringing me back here against my will?'

'You wouldn't really have chopped off our heads?' said Cy.

'Perhaps not. I might have had a half hundred horses trample you underfoot.'

'Why *half a hundred*?' asked Cy sitting down wearily on the couch. 'Two or three would do the job just as well.'

Shahr-Azad shook her head, and then leaned towards him. 'Tell me, O boy from the twenty-first century. Which is more terrifying? Two or three horses, or . . . half a hundred, rearing and plunging, their nostrils flecked with foam?'

'Half a hundred sounds more scary.'

'Exactly!' said Shahr-Azad. 'One must enhance the story.'

'Even though some of the things you say are not true?'

'But of course,' said Shahr-Azad. 'It is called hyperbole: some exaggeration to add flavour – a little embroidery here, a flash of colour there. To season a story with spices makes it a more appealing dish.'

'Well if you are going to punish me, go ahead,'

said Cy. 'The main reason I came back here was because I thought you might help me find my Dream Master.'

Shahr-Azad smiled. 'I cannot promise to find him, but I may be able to assist you. I fear I must speak with the genie.'

'I'll return to my own TimeSpace right away,' said Cy, 'and bring the bottle to you.'

'It would be best,' said Shahr-Azad smoothly, 'that we both journey to your Time. Who knows what could happen if you tried to travel there and back again on your own? Much could go amiss. Once there I will confront the genie.' She paused. 'You would, of course, grant me a small favour in return . . .'

'What?' Cy asked suspiciously.

'I would like to remain in your TimeSpace and see the TALENT TV competition—' and as Cy opened his mouth to say 'no', Shahr-Azad went on, 'It is something that I would like to do very much indeed.' She gave Cy a long look. 'So much have I wanted to witness this event, so much is my mind occupied with the thought of this, that I have not room for any other.'

Cy took a moment to think. He hadn't imagined it would be straightforward dealing with the Princess. She was obviously making her attendance at the TALENT TV competition a condition of helping him find the Dream Master. But the prospect of having Shahr-Azad living in his Time, even though it would only be for a couple of days, was distinctly worrying.

'What about the King? He expects you to tell him a story every night. You will be missed.'

Shahr-Azad shook her head. 'I will pretend to be unwell. The ladies in the palace will not betray me. The King will take the opportunity to go hunting for a few days.'

'If I agree that you can come with me then you must not behave as you did before,' said Cy.

'What did I do that was wrong?'

'You went wandering about,' said Cy.

'I could stay in your garage.'

'My friends and I are using the garage to rehearse our act for the competition.'

'I am very petite,' said Shahr-Azad. 'When anyone approaches I will conceal myself within the large straw basket.'

'I suppose it might work . . .' Cy hesitated. 'You must promise not to walk outside the garage.'

'I promise,' said Shahr-Azad. 'I will not walk outside the garage.' She lifted the magic carpet from the couch and unrolled it. 'Now I must collect a few things to bring with me.'

Cy looked at the magic carpet. 'Will there be room on that for a suitcase?'

'No suitcase,' said Shahr-Azad. 'A few items in one small box.' She went to a cupboard in the corner of the room, and took out an ornately carved wooden box. From the cupboard she also selected one or two shimmering scarves. Then she pressed a secret spring under the lid of the box. A hidden drawer slid open and Shahr-Azad placed the scarves inside.

It was almost dark when Cy and Shahr-Azad returned to the garage in Cy's Time and Space. The return journey was uneventful. The magic carpet knew the way and negotiated the strange territory of the other dimensions with ease, only bobbing and swaying occasionally as the currents lapped around it.

'It's nearly supper-time,' said Cy as the carpet came to rest with a gentle bump on the garage floor. 'I'll have to go. Otherwise Mum or Dad will come out looking for me.'

'One more day will give us more time to rest and consider what to do,' said Shahr-Azad as she settled down on her magic carpet for the night. 'Try to recall all the dreams that you have had since your Dream Master disappeared. Although you say he was not there with you, I believe he

149

must have been, in some way, trying to send you a message. Rest and reflect, Cy, and tomorrow night we will do battle with this cunning genie.'

# Chapter 20

All through the next day Cy had difficulty concentrating on his schoolwork. His mind kept returning to the questions Shahr-Azad had asked him about his dreams since the Dream Master had disappeared. Was the little man attempting to send him a message to say where he was? And if so what could it be? Was it something very obvious? Perhaps right in front of his nose and he couldn't see it?

Cy glanced up from his work. Mrs Chalmers was writing furiously on the white board with different coloured crayons. She was describing

parts of speech and Cy was really, really trying his best, but it was so hard to keep focused ... especially as a person was whispering to him.

'Cy. Cy.'

Cy looked around. All his classmates were listening intently to their teacher.

'Cy! Cy!'

Someone was definitely calling his name, softly but urgently. Cy glanced at Vicky and then at Chloe, who sat behind him. It wasn't them. Like everyone else in the room they were copying down the terms that Mrs Chalmers had written on the board.

'Psst. Cy! Cy!'

Cy's eyes drifted towards the classroom window. Then he gulped and his stomach turned over.

A bright red carpet was floating above the school playing fields! Sitting upon it was the Princess Shahr-Azad. She raised her arm and the magic carpet swooped low and hovered outside.

Cy recoiled from the window and flapped his hand to tell her to go away. Shahr-Azad waved merrily in return. Cy glanced around him. Had anyone else seen? His desk was right at the window and only he had his head raised. All his classmates had their heads down, writing furiously. Cy flapped his hand again. 'Go A-W-A-Y!' he spelled out silently.

Shahr-Azad beckoned to him. Cy scowled fiercely. Shahr-Azad stuck out her tongue. Cy turned his face so that he could not see the Princess. Perhaps if he ignored her she would get the message and leave. After a second or two he risked another glance. She had flipped the carpet over and was sitting on it upside down grinning cheekily at him!

'Cy! Cy!' His name was being called again. From a different direction.

'Cy! Cyrus Peters! Pay attention.'

'Whaaat?' Cy jolted round in his seat.

Mrs Chalmers was staring at him. 'You're off in a daydream,' she said. 'We were discussing language skills. Have you anything you'd like to add?'

'Ummm . . .'

'Have you followed any of this lesson at all, Cy?'

Behind him Chloe tittered. 'As if,' she said in a tiny voice.

Cy felt his face go red. His eyes flickered in the direction of the window.

'What is so interesting about the view from that window anyway?' said Mrs Chalmers.

Cy's head snapped back.

'Nothing,' he said. 'Nothing.'

But Mrs Chalmers was now at his desk. She was leaning right across to look out of the window! Wanting to see what had taken up his attention. Panic made Cy close his eyes tight. Make the Princess go away, he thought urgently. He opened his eyes again. The magic carpet was now a crimson blob high in the sky.

'Oh, I see what it is now,' said Mrs Chalmers.

'What do you see?' Cy's voice came out as a croak.

'It's the big balloon they've sent up to advertise the talent show at the weekend.' Mrs Chalmers drew away from the window. 'I know that the TALENT TV competition is being held the day after tomorrow and some of you intend to enter, but you must arrange all that outside class-time. At the moment we have to concentrate on schoolwork. And Cy . . .' His teacher gave him a severe look. 'Instead of letting your attention wander out of the window, perhaps you'd like to contribute?'

'C-C-C-Contribute?' Cy stuttered. He stared blankly at his teacher.

'Yes,' said Mrs Chalmers. 'We were discussing language skills. How language works. Have you anything that you'd like to say about that?'

Cy gazed up miserably at his teacher. 'Umm . . .

language . . .' Well he was living through a real experience on how words could be used to alter situations. That was how he'd lost his Dream Master and had to deal with a crazy princess. But he didn't feel that he could share that with everyone.

Mrs Chalmers shook her head and a little line of annoyance appeared between her eyes. 'I do wish you'd keep up, Cy. You, who have such a vivid imagination, would benefit from acquiring more language skills. It would enhance your stories so much.'

*Enhance.*

The word echoed in Cy's mind. Shahr-Azad had used the same word only last night.

'Hyperbole.' The word popped into Cy's head and straight out of his mouth.

Mrs Chalmers turned back with an expectant smile on her face. 'And?'

'Hyperbole,' Cy repeated. 'It's. It's fibs, but for a purpose . . . like, like, talking up a situation. Adding wild statements that can't be true to what you are saying. But doing it on purpose to make what you are saying sound more interesting or capture people's attention.'

'That's right, Cy!' said Mrs Chalmers. 'Hyperbole is deliberate exaggeration used for effect.'

Don't I know it, Cy thought to himself. I'm experiencing it right now. He spoke aloud. 'Stories need seasoning to enhance them.'

'Very good!' said Mrs Chalmers. 'I would say that almost sums up the whole lesson.'

Behind Cy Chloe made a clicking noise between her teeth. Then she whispered to Eddie, 'We need to do something to take him down a peg.'

After school that afternoon when Cy returned home with his Grampa they found the living room unusually messy. Grampa picked up the TV magazine from among a pile of newspapers scattered on the floor. 'You must have all gone out in a rush this morning,' he said. 'Look, the television's been left on.'

Cy stopped on his way into the kitchen. The television was tuned to a chat show. It was one of those ones where a person called Valensa or Morticia asks guests to confront personal problems. Cy wasn't a fan of that type of show. He couldn't imagine telling everyone all about yourself.

'Yecchh!' he said. 'Who would watch that?'

From outside the kitchen door Cy heard hurried footsteps and saw a shadow pass the kitchen window. It was Shahr-Azad! As well as flying about on her magic carpet today, the Princess must have been watching TV inside his house!

Cy made a couple of sandwiches for himself and Grampa and then went out to the garage. Surrounded by empty crisp packets and chocolate biscuit wrappers Shahr-Azad was sitting, serenely braiding her hair.

'Don't pretend that you've been quietly behaving yourself all day,' Cy said angrily. 'I know that you've been watching television and whizzing about on your magic carpet.'

'I did take a short outing . . . around and about,' said Shahr-Azad licking the inside of the bag of cheese and onion flavoured crisps. 'This taste is superb,' she said.

'What do you think you are doing?' Cy demanded. 'You promised me that you would stay in the garage.'

'I did not,' said Shahr-Azad.

'Yes, you did! You said that you wouldn't go outside.'

'You made me promise not to *walk* outside. And I didn't. I flew.'

Cy snorted. 'That's, that's . . .'

'Pedantic?' suggested Shahr-Azad.

'You were supposed to be thinking about how to get my Dream Master back, not flying your magic carpet about the school grounds, gorging on food, and watching daytime TV and—' Cy stopped as a thought occurred to him. 'How did you get out of the garage and into my house? They were both locked up.'

'Tsss!' said Shahr-Azad. 'That was easy.' She took the old key that was Cy's prop for the magic show and wrapped it in one of the scarves from her box. To Cy's amazement the end softened and bent in her hand. Shahr-Azad slipped the pliable mixture into the door lock, where it solidified, then she turned the newly formed key and the door unlocked.

'You mustn't go out again,' Cy pleaded with her. 'If someone sees you it will cause all sorts of trouble. My teacher, Mrs Chalmers, caught a glimpse as you flew off this afternoon. Luckily you were so far away that she thought it was the TALENT TV hot-air balloon.'

'I noticed something hanging in the sky above the town. A large round object. What is it?' Shahr-Azad asked curiously.

'It's a large inflatable. The TV company are using it for publicity.' said Cy.

'What is this "publicity"?'

'It's to advertise their show. Tell people about it.'

'I see how effective that is. Being so high in the

sky, then it can be seen by many,' said Shahr-Azad. There was a thoughtful look in her eye.

'Yes,' Cy went on impatiently. 'Now listen. You *must* stay hidden in the Ali-Baba basket when my friends are here practising our act. Then, after they've gone, we can try to find my Dream Master.'

Shahr-Azad bowed her head obediently. She lifted the lid of the straw basket and climbed inside.

'Until then,' she said.

# Chapter 21

After Cy's friends had left Shahr-Azad got out of the straw basket and Cy brought her the little bottle from the window-sill which contained the genie.

Shahr-Azad studied the contents for a moment or two. 'Strange,' she murmured. 'You described the genie to me as wearing green with gold earrings yet among these grains are also blue and black.' She raised her head to Cy. 'Tell me your dreams of the last few days.'

'One was about the sea. I was nearly swallowed by a whale. It was as though I was going down a

tunnel.'

'Wherever your Dream Master is, he will be dreamweaving for you, but I fear he's being held under the most constrained circumstances. Go on.'

'Another time I was in a cave.'

'Alone?'

'No.' Cy thought for a moment. 'There is always someone else there but I cannot see them or . . .'

'Or?'

'Or hear them speak.'

Shahr-Azad put her head to one side. 'That is interesting . . . Now tell me, what did you say to the genie immediately before your Dream Master disappeared?'

'I said I wanted him to vanish.'

'What were your exact words?' asked Shahr-Azad. 'Be specific. Your Dream Master may have told you that words have great potency and power.'

Cy thought about this. How the two bullies Chloe and Eddie used words to put people down and how hurtful that was.

'And genies can be very literal,' Shahr-Azad went on. She smiled at Cy's blank look. 'They will do *exactly* what you say. Give you *precisely* what you request.'

'I think I said, "go away". No it wasn't that, not

quite . . .' Cy shook his head hopelessly. 'I can't remember exactly.'

'From what you have told me this genie sounds very lazy.' Shahr-Azad spoke slowly. 'He would take the easiest course open to him.'

Cy recalled that he had been arguing with his Dream Master in the prison cell. The little man had lost his temper and Cy had shouted at him. 'I said, I said, "I wish you'd just go, put a sock in it and disappear", something like that.'

'Aha!' The Princess clapped her hands. 'Now it becomes clearer.' Her eyes sparkled. 'Let us summon this troublesome genie.' She turned to Cy. 'I beg of you, no matter what happens, be silent until I bid you speak.'

When Cy nodded in agreement Shahr-Azad drew the stopper from the bottle and gently blew into the neck. 'Arise O Wonderful Genie. The Princess Shahr-Azad requests your presence.'

At once a great plume of smoke swirled from the bottle. It filled the garage and the figure of the genie assembled.

'What do *you* want?' He folded his arms and looked down at Shahr-Azad. Then he narrowed his eyes. '*The* Princess Shahr-Azad?'

'It is indeed I, O Illustrious One,' Shahr-Azad kneeled down and raised both her hands in supplication, 'come to beg a favour from thee.'

'Three only.' The genie tutted. 'The person who opens the bottle gets three, max. So get on with it. I don't have all day.'

'It is gracious of you to grant me even this small portion of your time.'

'I don't think people realize,' said the genie, 'how busy I am. Rushing here, hurrying there, doing everybody's bidding. Fetching and carrying, never a moment to call my own . . .'

That was totally untrue, Cy thought. He knew for certain that this genie had not done anything for the last few days, because he had been inside a bottle sitting on the window-sill of Cy's garage. Cy opened his mouth to tell Shahr-Azad this.

'He's been doing nothing for—'

As Shahr-Azad put a warning finger to her lips Cy remembered that he was supposed to have kept quiet.

'Aha!' cried the genie, spying Cy crouched behind the Ali-Baba basket. 'You are in league with this annoying boy!' His figure expanded and he filled the whole of the roof space of the garage. 'I should have known that I was not rid of him or his Dream Master.'

'This is the subject that I wish to discuss,' said Shahr-Azad.

'And I suppose,' the genie said casually, 'you also want to talk about where the little fellow is exactly?'

'Yes,' said Shahr-Azad. 'That is something I very much want to discuss.'

'Gotcha!' said the genie. 'You said "I wish" and "I want". Two wishes down!'

Shahr-Azad bit her lip.

'I have outwitted the Princess Shahr-Azad!' The genie crowed in delight. 'That doesn't happen very often!'

Shahr-Azad lowered her head, but Cy saw that there was a satisfied look in her eyes. By allowing the genie to think he had tricked her into losing her first two wishes she had made him much more willing to agree to grant her third.

'Therefore grant me my last wish without further trouble.' Shahr-Azad spoke firmly. 'Restore Cy's Dream Master to him, now, this moment, here in this garage, as he was before.'

'Oh, all right.' The genie yawned. 'I'm tired out now. And it *was* getting very crowded in there.' The genie pointed at the bottle and then chortled at Cy's stunned look. 'Your little chum was right under your nose all the time.'

The form of the genie dematerialized slowly and trickled into the neck of the bottle. As the genie disappeared coloured sand came spraying out of the bottle to pile up in a great mound in front of Cy and Shahr-Azad. Cy replaced the stopper, put the bottle containing the genie on the window-sill and turned round. The grains in the middle of the floor fused together until finally before them stood an apoplectic little figure. A large woolly sock was jammed between his lips completely filling his mouth. His eyes stood out and his face was suffused purple.

Cy and Shahr-Azad stepped back a few paces.

'Omigosh!' said Cy. 'Omigollygosh!'

Shahr-Azad reached out and very gently removed the sock from the mouth of the Dream Master.

Then she and Cy quickly covered their ears with both hands . . .

# Chapter 22

After school on Friday Cy went straight to the field with his Grampa. They had to queue along with lots of young people to get past the turnstiles. Cy wanted to check out the venue where he and his friends were scheduled to appear tomorrow. Some performance heats were already being held and a line had formed outside the marquee where registration was taking place. Cy stopped to talk with a couple of girls from the year below him who had put together a dance routine. Little groups stood about reciting lines or holding impromptu rehearsals.

Suddenly a great 'Ohhh' went up from the field and everyone turned their faces up to look at the sky.

The hot-air balloon was descending, trailing a great shower of fireworks and soap bubbles. From the basket a small figure waved regally.

'Shahr-Azad!' cried Cy.

He raced across the field as the balloon came to rest next to the cordoned-off judges' enclosure. Shahr-Azad climbed out and was escorted away from the restricted area by some of the officials. As Cy waited for Shahr-Azad to come out of the staff area he heard a few people talking.

'She must have hidden in the little basket attached to the bottom of the balloon.'

'Well done, you,' someone said to Shahr-Azad as she came to join Cy. 'Wish I'd thought of it.'

Shahr-Azad smiled happily and waved her hand.

'Good publicity trick,' said another person.

'I don't think so,' said a voice Cy recognized. It was Chloe, her face twisted in jealousy. 'She didn't queue up for hours to get in like everybody else. So that's cheating. It's given her an unfair advantage.'

'Yes,' said Eddie who was standing beside her. 'We thought of doing that. Except we read the posters and the balloon was advertised as an *unmanned* flight.'

'But I am a woman not a man,' said Shahr-Azad. 'I broke no law.'

'It was deceitful,' Eddie accused her.

'It was audacious,' Shahr-Azad replied.

'Show-off,' said Chloe.

'Artful,' countered Shahr-Azad.

Cy grinned. This should be fun, watching Chloe and Eddie try to outwit Shahr-Azad in a word competition.

'Smarty-pants,' said Chloe.

Shahr-Azad lifted one eyebrow. 'Resourceful.'

'You think you are a real clever-clogs,' said Eddie.

'I believe I am astute,' Shahr-Azad replied.

Chloe pushed her face up close to Shahr-Azad. She mimicked Shahr-Azad's voice nastily. 'Well, *I* believe that you are underhand, dishonest and two-faced.'

Shahr-Azad laughed in delight. 'This is an excellent competition. I like it!' She placed her hand under her chin and puzzled for a moment. 'On the contrary, my actions were crafty, inventive, wily and clever.'

A few people stopped to listen. With a deep feeling of apprehension Cy saw that his class teacher Mrs Chalmers was among them. 'Those are a couple of my pupils there,' Cy heard Mrs

Chalmers comment to the person beside her. 'Such magnificent use of vocabulary.'

That's typical, thought Cy. The Mean Machines always seemed to get away with their nastiness. Mrs Chalmers didn't realize that Eddie and Chloe were being horrible to Shahr-Azad.

'You're just a know-all!' said Eddie.

Shahr-Azad made a graceful salaam to him. 'I thank you,' she replied.

'Well done!' A voice from the crowd called out.

Cy pulled on Shahr-Azad's sleeve. She shook him off. 'Beat. It,' she said. 'If this is part of the TALENT TV competition, then I am going to win.'

'Are you a friend of that young lady?' Mrs Chalmers asked Cy.

'Well, yes. No. Yes.'

Mrs Chalmers smiled at Cy. 'Which is it?' she asked.

'I sort of know her,' Cy mumbled.

'She's not local, is she?' said Mrs Chalmers. 'Did you meet her at the youth club community centre?'

'Uh,' Cy grunted.

'Is she from the family of one of the asylum-seekers?'

'I never actually asked her,' said Cy. 'But I suppose she is, kind of.' Both he and Mrs Chalmers stopped speaking as the exchange between

169

Shahr-Azad and the Mean Machines continued.

'You've been underhand,' Chloe told Shahr-Azad.

'Slick,' declared Shahr-Azad.

'More like shifty!' said Eddie.

'I'd say shrewd,' Shahr-Azad replied.

'Sneaky,' said Chloe.

'Subtle,' said Shahr-Azad.

'Sly!'

'Smart!'

'Slippery!'

'Skilful!'

Eddie and Chloe looked at each other.

'Gifted,' continued Shahr-Azad. 'Ingenious. Dextrous. Expert.'

'Er...' said Eddie. He looked at Chloe. She shook her head.

Shahr-Azad clapped her hands. 'I win!' she cried. 'I win.'

There was a burst of cheering and a round of applause. Some of the crowd stopped to speak to Shahr-Azad and admire her clothes. By the time Cy pushed his way through to her an official with a clipboard was taking her details. 'You don't need to wait in line to get an entry form,' he was saying. 'I'll give you one of these. I can recognize original talent when I see it. Now tell me, what would you like to enter the competition as?'

'As myself,' said Shahr-Azad.

'Yup, honey. But what is it you actually do?'

'A princess does not need to *do* anything,' said Shahr-Azad loftily.

'Absolutely.' The man laughed. 'But help me out here. What kind of slot are you looking for? What's your specific talent?'

'Storytelling,' said Shahr-Azad. 'I am a Storyteller.'

'Excellent. Excellent. We haven't got one of those.' He wrote on the form. 'Now what's your act title?'

'My title? I am a princess.'

The man stopped with his pen above the entry form. 'Ummm . . . Can you give yourself a stage name? Something short, with a bit of a punch.'

'Kerpow?' suggested Shahr-Azad.

'Sorry?' The man blinked. 'Tell you what, you fill in the rest yourself and hand it in.'

As the man gave the entry form to Shahr-Azad, Cy took it and dragged Shahr-Azad to one side. 'What are you up to?' he demanded. 'I told you I'd take you here *tomorrow* when the competition is on.'

Shahr-Azad pouted. 'Yes, but if I'd waited until tomorrow I would not have been given a form by that kind gentleman.'

'That "kind gentleman" is a greaseball,' said Cy.

'He is Greaseball?' repeated Shahr-Azad.

'Yes,' said Cy. 'A slimy greaseball who wants you to do something for his benefit. I don't think it's a good idea for you to enter the competition.'

'Why ever not?' Mrs Chalmers had overheard what Cy was saying. She spoke to Shahr-Azad. 'It is so interesting to hear stories from other cultures. What name do you call yourself?'

'Shahr-Azad,' said Shahr-Azad.

'Scheherazade!' Mrs Chalmers repeated. 'What a neat idea to call yourself after the teller of the Arabian Nights. I'll bet Cy suggested that. Here, I'll hand your entry form in for you.' And before Cy could stop her, Mrs Chalmers took the slip of paper from Shahr-Azad and walked off towards the registration marquee.

# Chapter 23

Cy went out to the garage early the next morning. He wanted to get his props together and take Shahr-Azad to the field before anyone else was about. He found Shahr-Azad arranging her scarves about her face and head.

'This is a crazy idea,' the Dream Master grizzled at Cy. 'You don't know what mischief she'll get up to.'

'I had to promise to bring her with me today so that she would help me find you,' said Cy. 'You wouldn't want to have stayed inside that bottle

with a sock in your mouth for ever, would you?'

Cy's Dream Master glared at him. 'And whose fault was it that I ended up inside the bottle in the first place?' he asked bitterly.

'You yourself were partly to blame for that,' said Cy. 'Anyway let's get organized. I want to be on my way before other people are up and about.'

Unknown to Cy other people were already up and about. The Mean Machines, Eddie and Chloe, angry at having been put down in front of everyone yesterday, were at this moment outside Cy's garage looking for revenge.

'I can hear voices,' Chloe whispered to Eddie. 'Cy must be in there already with his friends. We've arrived too late to mess up any of their things.' Her face clouded as she realized that her plan to wreck Cy's magic act would be thwarted.

'The window's open,' said Eddie. 'Let's have a look inside.'

The Mean Machines climbed quietly onto the waste bins lined up along the side of the garage and tried to peer in the window.

'There's some old sheet pinned up here that's stopping me seeing anything,' said Chloe. She reached her hand in to try to pull aside the curtain. Her fingers connected with the little glass bottle that held the genie.

'What have you got?' Eddie asked Chloe as she withdrew her hand holding the bottle.

'One of his silly magic potions.' Chloe turned to show it to Eddie but, as she did, the bin lid slipped to one side and so did she. Still clutching the bottle she slid to the ground with a clatter.

The Mean Machines scrambled to their feet as the garage door opened.

'What are you two doing here?' Cy asked. 'You've no right to be in my garden.'

'We, we—' Eddie began.

'What have you got in your hand?' said Cy, catching sight of the bottle. 'Omigosh!' he said.

'We came to wish you luck,' said Chloe innocently.

'Give me that bottle and go away. It's bad luck to wish someone luck before a performance,' said Cy.

'So you *do* catch on occasionally,' Eddie sneered.

'Yes,' said Chloe. She threw the bottle in the air, made as if to grab it, then opened her hands wide. 'I wish your act today is truly spectacular,' she said sarcastically as the bottle fell and shattered at her feet.

She and Eddie ran out of the garden and along the street. Neither of them noticed the thin column of smoke which trailed from the broken pieces of glass and drifted after them.

'Omigosh!' said Cy. 'Omigollygosh!'

Cy raced inside the garage, stuffed his props and his dad's old dinner jacket into his rucksack, calling to Shahr-Azad as he did so. 'Chloe has released the genie from the bottle! It's following them along the street. Come on!'

The Dream Master wrapped himself up in his dreamcloak. 'I suppose I'll have to come with you,' he grumbled. 'Hopefully I'll go unnoticed among the crowd that will be there today.'

By the time Cy got into the street there was no sign of Eddie and Chloe.

'What shall we do?' asked Cy in alarm.

'Let us go to the place of the competition,' said Shahr-Azad. 'It is more than likely that is where we will find them and the genie. But wait!' She ran back into the garage to fetch the little enamel teapot. 'We need a container for the genie when we find him,' she explained to Cy.

Cy took his piece of dreamsilk from the teapot and tucked it into his trouser pocket.

'Think of what might happen if Chloe knows that there is a genie that will grant her wishes!' said Cy, a panicky note in his voice.

'She will have to take the consequences then.' Shahr-Azad spoke grimly. 'In some parts of Arabia it is seen as a curse – to obtain all that your heart desires.'

'Indeed,' the Dream Master muttered in Cy's ear. 'As you yourself know, Button Brain. You must be careful what you wish for.'

Cy, Shahr-Azad and the Dream Master ran as fast as they could to the competition field. The whole area was filling up with people who had early morning slots. Cy saw two girls from Lauren's school who were expert gymnasts. They were already in their costumes and practising hand-stands and somersaults. A group of pupils from his school passed by carrying their musical instruments.

'There they are!' cried Shahr-Azad.

Eddie and Chloe were walking between two tents. A dark cloud rolled above their heads.

'I will try to warn them in a way they will under-stand,' said Shahr-Azad. She ran forward and stepped in front of the Mean Machines. 'Listen up, wise guys,' she said.

' "*Wise guys*?" ' Cy mouthed the words at the Dream Master behind her back. 'That's not language from Ancient Arabia.'

'Sounds like American gangster slang,' said the Dream Master. 'I blame all those old comics that you've got lying about your bedroom floor.'

'We need some talk-time pronto,' Shahr-Azad told Eddie and Chloe.

'Get lost,' Chloe told her. 'We're due to go on soon. You're in our way.'

'Yeah, beat it,' Eddie chimed in. 'We don't have time to talk to cheats.'

'I'm going to blow this geezer to kingdom come,' declared Shahr-Azad. She took up an aggressive stand, arms folded across her chest.

Cy's mouth gaped open. His Dream Master peered out nervously from behind him.

'She might know how to do karate,' Eddie said to Chloe, his voice less confident now.

'Forget karate!' snarled Shahr-Azad. 'Get ready for some Killer Kickboxing.' She spun on one heel, her leg shot out and her foot almost reached Eddie's chin. He leaped back.

'I don't know about this,' Eddie turned to Chloe.

'Oh, don't be such a wimp,' said Chloe. She pushed Eddie aside. 'I'll deal with her if you can't.'

'Come ahead. Punk,' Shahr-Azad sneered. 'Make my day.'

Chloe took one step forward. Shahr-Azad took two steps forward to meet her. Chloe hesitated, stepped back, then she and Eddie turned and ran.

'KERPOW!' Shahr-Azad shouted after the two bullies. 'ZAM! SPLAT!'

Cy grabbed Shahr-Azad's sleeve. 'Why are you talking like that?'

'These words are in your comic books,' said Shahr-Azad in a puzzled voice. 'It is what the good guys say.'

'Yes, but—' Cy began.

'Can we get on?' snapped the Dream Master. 'It may have escaped your attention but Chloe and Eddie are about to do their act supported by a slightly confused genie.'

'Can't you do anything to stop the genie giving Chloe what she wants?' Cy asked Shahr-Azad as the three of them hurried into the performance tent.

Shahr-Azad shook her head. 'I cannot,' she said. 'And neither can the genie. It is Kismet. He must grant the three wishes. Although how he interprets the request . . . is entirely up to him.'

Cy didn't have long to wait to find out how the genie was going to interpret any request that Chloe made. Shahr-Azad had decided that it would be best if they were as close to the stage as possible so that she could keep an eye on things, which meant that Cy had a close-up view of what happened.

Eddie and Chloe were the third act to come on.

'Chloe and Eddie!' the announcer bawled at the

179

top of his voice. 'I want you all to give a big welcome to these young people who are going to sing a medley of popular songs.'

The audience clapped loudly as Chloe strode onto the stage. Eddie lagged a bit behind her fiddling with the buttons of his jacket.

'I wish you'd hurry up!' Chloe whispered impatiently at him.

Immediately Eddie's head jerked up, then he leaped forward, galloped to the front of the stage, grabbed the mike and began singing their song as fast as he could.

'What are you doing?' cried Chloe.

Eddie ignored her. His whole body convulsed as he went into their dance routine at top speed, stepping about the stage in a mad frenzy. Then he belted out the last two verses of the song and finished up with a great flourishing bow.

'Brilliant!' Shahr-Azad stood up to lead the applause.

'Next!' shouted the Dream Master.

Eddie dashed off the stage, danced out the door, and round the back of the tent.

'Why did you do that?' screamed Chloe, racing after him.

'YoutoldmetohurryupandIcouldn'tstop.' Eddie looked around wildly. His feet danced a few more steps, slowed down and then stopped, whereupon Eddie collapsed onto the grass. 'I couldn't help myself,' he sobbed.

'You've ruined everything,' moaned Chloe. 'It's all spoiled. I wanted our act to be the coolest thing here.'

Above the heads of the two bullies a large grey cloud changed to white and cold snowflakes began to fall gently down upon them . . .

# Chapter 24

As it came closer to the time of his own act Cy's stomach was churning with dread and awful anticipation. Why had he ever thought that he could do this? He was far too inept to perform magic tricks. He didn't know whether to be comforted or worried by the fact that his friends were tense and jittery too. They'd had to report to their performance tent an hour before their act time, and since then they had all been running backwards and forwards to the toilets.

Suddenly Lauren appeared and thumped Cy on the back. 'Go to it, bro,' she said. 'I won't wish you

luck 'cos that's bad luck, but you know what I mean.'

'You too,' said Cy, watching her as she swung away to join the audience queue to get into the tent, humming '*Go, Girl, Go . . . Oh, Oh, Oh, Oh . . .*' He caught sight of his mum and dad already waiting in the line and they both gave him the thumbs up sign.

'It's only a bit of fun,' Cy's dad had said last night. He'd looked at Cy seriously as he spoke. 'Remember that, and you'll be fine.'

Mum hadn't said anything. She'd been a bit distracted, trying to find Cy's trainers . . .

Vicky peered out from behind the stage curtain. 'The tent is pretty full,' she said, 'but it's mainly our friends and family. Oh no!' she said then. 'Look!'

Cy looked to where she was pointing. Eddie and Chloe had slipped in and sat down. They looked a bit wet but had obviously stopped arguing with each other. Close behind the Mean Machines drifted an almost transparent mist. There was a faint rumble in the air and a wisp of smoke curled above Chloe's head.

'Sounds like a bit of thunder,' said Basra. 'Hope the rain holds off.'

It wasn't thunder. The vague ball of mist coiled upwards and hung above the audience.

Below the genie Chloe spoke under her breath to Eddie. 'This is going to be so funny. Putting those old vegetables in Innis's juggling bag when he was in the loo was a brainwave.'

'I can't wait to see Basra's face when he discovers the inside of his cannon is blocked,' said Eddie.

Someone else had seen the entrance of the Mean Machines and the genie. Shahr-Azad nudged the Dream Master in their seats behind them. 'I know this genie has not treated you well, O mighty Dream Lord, but for Cy's sake . . .'

The Dream Master fixed his gaze on the top of the tent. Then he stood up and opened his dream-cloak. The smoke from the top of the tent spiralled down towards them. From under the dreamcloak the form of the genie took shape and he emerged, shaking himself. A mother in the seat next to Shahr-Azad took her child by the hand and moved to another row.

'I'm totally knackered,' said the genie, flopping into the vacant seat. 'I've got to follow that odious girl around until I fulfil all of her three wishes. And was she pleased earlier when I gave her exactly what she asked for with two of them? No she was not. She is a very discontented young lady.'

'Has she made her three wishes?' asked Shahr-Azad.

'Yes,' said the genie. 'Although her very first wish I have yet to grant. When she released me from the bottle by letting it smash on the ground she said that she hoped the boy Cy's act today would be "truly spectacular". I have still to arrange for that to happen.' He peered around the tent and caught sight of Cy and his friends being ushered onto the stage. 'Oh there he is,' he said. 'I'd better do something about that now.' The genie raised his hand.

'Not yet.' Shahr-Azad placed a restraining hand on the genie's arm. 'Not yet,' she murmured.

'Another thing,' the genie moaned on. 'My bottle has been smashed. What am I supposed to do about that? Eh? Where do I go to put my feet up and have a bit of shut-eye now?'

Shahr-Azad took the little teapot from under her jacket. 'I have brought you a new resting place,' she told him. 'For when your work is done here.'

'A teapot?' The genie regarded her disdainfully. 'Then I'd be known as the Genie of the Teapot! I don't think so.'

'I didn't see it as a teapot,' Shahr-Azad spoke softly. Her great eyes darkened and her voice became as smooth as satin. 'When I look at this . . .' she held the teapot up and turned it in her hands, '. . . I behold a lamp. A *magic* lamp.'

185

'Really?' The genie peered more closely. 'Oh . . . yes I see what you mean.'

'You would be the Genie of the *Lamp*. *The* Genie of the *Magic* Lamp.'

'Mmmmm.' The genie preened himself. 'It *does* have a certain ring to it, doesn't it?'

Shahr-Azad smiled in agreement. The Dream Master nodded furiously. All three turned their heads to face the front as the 'Magical Mixture' act was announced.

Basra began by firing off his cannon full of confetti. At least that was what he intended to do . . . Basra pulled the lever and stood clear. The cannon made a small *phut!* and coughed out a few feathers. Basra bent down to examine the mechanism anxiously, while Vicky mounted her mono-cycle and started to pedal around the stage.

'It would be such a laugh,' Chloe muttered to Eddie, 'if Vicky fell right off that bike.'

The genie exchanged a look with Shahr-Azad. 'You see how this child's mind works?'

'It might not be totally inappropriate,' Shahr-Azad said thoughtfully.

On stage Innis reached into his prop bag, but instead of his special soft juggling balls he found a cabbage, a cauliflower, and a turnip. He carried on gamely, but the turnip was very old and rotten, and he could not keep all the items in the air simultaneously. He moved to one side.

Seeing his predicament Cy hurriedly began his part of the show. 'I will now make something vanish,' he said hesitantly.

'I wish something would go splat,' said Chloe viciously.

The genie raised an eyebrow and Shahr-Azad smiled. On stage Cy was pretending to wrap the old key up in the red spotted scarf. From the back of the tent Shahr-Azad took her scarf between her fingers and wafted it gently to and fro. The next moment the elastic snapped up. The key boinged into the air and Cy had to duck his head to avoid being struck in the face. He stumbled backwards, almost colliding with Vicky. She managed to keep upright by reaching out and grabbing hold of Innis's hair.

'Er, er,' Cy stuttered glancing round wildly. 'I'll now burst this balloon. I mean I won't. That is, it won't. Burst that is. But I will. Burst. The balloon, I mean. Not me. Later. In a minute.'

Cy looked around for help. Innis was gamely throwing vegetables in the air one by one with Vicky clutching his head. Basra was peering down the barrel of the cannon.

Cy lifted up the balloon and slowly slid the long

skewer inside from end to end. There was some applause, but it was mainly, Cy saw, from their families who had come along to support them. He withdrew the skewer and prepared to burst the balloon holding it high by the trail of coloured ribbons. Meanwhile Vicky regained her balance and resumed cycling. Basra whispered urgently, 'I think I've got rid of the blockage now. Let's go for the finale.'

One of Princess Shahr-Azad's scarves wafted to and fro, and she winked at the genie. Suddenly, metres and metres of ribbon unravelled from both Cy's sleeves, cascaded down his legs and began to pile up on the floor around his feet. He stumbled around the stage almost colliding with Vicky who was going backwards and forwards on her trick cycle.

Basra's cannon still wouldn't work. He got to his knees in front of it and stuck his hand down the barrel. Then he drew back with a very strange expression on his face. A pigeon hopped out. Basra let out a yelp as it tried to peck him. The bird flew up and landed on Cy's head. Then Basra's cannon exploded and a blizzard of bird feathers poured out. He sneezed and flailed his arms about helplessly. At the same moment Cy tripped forwards into the huge mound of coloured ribbons, Vicky wobbled horribly and cannoned into Innis. The rotten turnip sailed through the air and landed *splat!* in Chloe's lap spattering both her and Eddie with rancid mush. Vicky fell off her cycle, and, dragging Innis with her, they both ended in a heap on top of Cy.

The four friends disentangled themselves and stood up. The tent was rocking with laughter. It was too much humiliation and disappointment, thought Cy. He saw Eddie and Chloe mopping up goo from their clothes but still jeering at their terrible performance. His face flared with shame. And then Cy saw and heard something else. The crowd were *cheering*, not jeering. The audience were clapping furiously. Led by Grampa and Mrs Turner, everyone stood up and began to shout 'Encore! Encore!'

'That was so clever, Cy,' said Vicky afterwards, 'putting all that extra ribbon up your sleeve and having it stream out like that.'

'And you too,' said Cy. 'To do a trick fall from a mono-cycle isn't easy.'

'I didn't mean it to happen quite like that,' said Vicky truthfully.

'Yes, but you got up and took the bow,' said Innis. 'That was really smart, Vicky.'

'It's the sign of a true performer,' said Basra. 'Able to ad-lib.'

'I can see how you fixed the ribbon and the feathers,' Vicky said to Cy, 'but I don't know how you managed the dove.'

'I'm not too sure about that myself,' said Cy. His mind sought desperately for a solution as his friends waited for an answer. 'I think maybe Grampa helped out a bit. One of his friends has access to a lot of birds.'

'Oh that's right,' said Innis. 'Mrs Turner's neighbour keeps pigeons.'

Fortunately at this moment Cy's mum and dad interrupted and Cy didn't have to say any more.

'Congratulations, son,' said Cy's dad. 'You should rename your act "Magical Mayhem". I don't know how you stage-managed that finale at the end, but it was brilliant.'

Cy's mum was still wiping away tears of laughter. 'It was *so* funny. I thought I was never going to stop laughing. Excellent comic timing. You must have practised so hard to have Basra disappear in a storm of feathers, Vicky tumble off on top of Innis, and you trip up into the piles of ribbon, all at exactly the same time.'

Cy and his friends looked at each other.

'Hilarious,' they agreed.

# Chapter 25

**A**s Cy had expected Shahr-Azad had a huge attendance for her storytelling session.

Word of her unusual arrival on the field had got round and rumours had spread that she was a member of a European Royal Family appearing incognito. Cy had trouble finding her and the Dream Master afterwards, eventually tracking them down outside one of the TV caravans. Shahr-Azad was in conversation with Greaseball.

'You'll be big,' Greaseball was telling her as the Dream Master stood to one side chewing on his beard.

'Big?' said Shahr-Azad. 'I am petite.'

'By "big", I mean—' Greaseball waved his hand in the air. 'Well, big, anyway. Your stories are fabulous. Probably need a bit of work on them here and there...'

'Work?' said Shahr-Azad. 'What kind of "work" do you mean?'

'Nip and tuck.'

'Nip? And Tuck? Who are Nip and Tuck?'

Greaseball gave Shahr-Azad a puzzled look. 'You've lost me there, honey.'

'Are they characters? This Nip and Tuck?'

'Oh right, I get it. Fun-eee.' Greaseball made a face. 'Or not.' He muttered under his breath, 'Why is it everyone thinks they can do comedy? Take my advice, honey,' he said in a louder voice. 'Leave the jokes to the experts.'

'You think I am not an expert?' There was a slight edge to Shahr-Azad's voice.

'Honey, we all got to accept that there's room for improvement.'

Cy noticed that the temperature had fallen by a few degrees. 'Explain, please,' Shahr-Azad demanded icily.

'Your stories do need a bit of tweaking,' Greaseball blundered on.

'Tweaking? What is tweaking?'

'A little bit of this and that.'

Shahr-Azad looked puzzled. She turned to Cy. 'What is this person talking about?'

Cy shrugged. 'Dunno.' He often found the way that adults spoke confusing. They used what his dad called buzz words like 'achieving potential' and 'turnaround time'. It was almost as though they didn't want you to know what they meant.

'We're marketing for a modern audience. We need some good sound bites,' said Greaseball.

'What is a "sound bite" exactly?' asked Shahr-Azad.

'It is a sentence that has instant appeal. A phrase that is exciting.'

'You think my stories are not exciting?' asked Shahr-Azad in what Cy now recognized as a decidedly dangerous tone of voice.

Cy and the Dream Master stepped back a pace.

'I wouldn't go there,' Cy said to Greaseball.

'Not even halfway there,' the Dream Master added.

'You must admit they could do with a bit more *oomph*,' Greaseball blundered on. 'Our script editors will be able to spruce them up, make them more interesting.'

*'Make my stories more interesting!'*

The Dream Master and Cy hurriedly backed

away as the full two million candle-power force of Shahr-Azad's wrath exploded into Greaseball's face.

'*Make my stories more interesting!* My stories,' she shrieked, 'could not *be* more interesting. I have entertained the King of all Arabia for one thousand nights. Moguls of China, sultans of the Ottoman Empire, caliphs from Baghdad and maharajahs of India *beg* to be included in my stories. *I* created flying carpets, horses that could ride wind and water, magical castles and caverns full of treasure.'

'Honey—' Greaseball attempted to interrupt. But there was no stopping an angry princess.

'And *you*, you insignificant ant, you have the effrontery to advise *me* to make my stories more interesting!'

'It-it-it-it was only a suggestion,' stuttered Greaseball.

'I can conjure up necromancers and magicians. On my command, genies appear.'

'Not literally,' reasoned Greaseball.

'No?' said Shahr-Azad. She reached under he jacket to take out the little enamel teapot.

'No!' cried Cy and the Dream Master together.

Shahr-Azad dropped her hand.

'We could offer you your own show,' said Greaseball in a wheedling tone of voice.

'She's got her own show,' said Cy. 'Come on,' he spoke urgently to Shahr-Azad.

'Who are you?' asked Greaseball.

'Never you mind,' snapped the Dream Master. 'Who are you?'

'The man with the money,' replied the producer. He slid his arm around Shahr-Azad's shoulder. 'I can get you the best merchandising deals.'

Shahr-Azad looked at his arm as if it were some particularly repellent snake. Greaseball removed it. 'Uh, let me tell you the kind of cash I'm talking about.'

'Cash?' said Shahr-Azad.

'Money. Spondoolicks. The Readies.' And as Shahr-Azad still looked blank. 'You could buy things. Clothes. Cars. Go on world tours.'

'I would like to see the world,' said Shahr-Azad.

'You will,' he assured her. 'You'll be big in the old U.S. of A.'

'Where is that, precisely?' asked Shahr-Azad.

Greaseball turned to Cy. 'Is she for real?'

'She's led a sheltered life,' Cy muttered. 'Doesn't go out much.'

'I can see it now,' said Greaseball. ' "*Shahr-Azad – the Movie*". We'll use animation.'

'Animation?' said Shahr-Azad suspiciously.

'Or special effects,' Greaseball rambled on.

'We'll get top actors for voice-overs. What is that mythical bird you mentioned? The one with the huge wingspan and the great claws that tears people's heads off?

'The roc?'

'That's the one. We'll create a roc using computer graphics.'

'But it is not mythical,' said Shahr-Azad. 'I myself have seen one.'

'Yeah, right,' said Greaseball. He looked at Shahr-Azad for a moment and then continued. 'So we'll create that anyway, with the flying castles and some of the other things you mentioned.'

'But it is the listener to the storyteller, the reader of the book who creates,' said Shahr-Azad.

'But this way we save them the effort. We do it for them.'

'You steal the story from them.'

'Oh no,' said Greaseball. 'We kind of *interpret* your stories in our way.'

'But, in truth, eventually…' Shahr-Azad spoke very slowly, 'they are not finally only my stories. I mean they *are* my stories, but as soon as they are spoken they belong to everyone. Stories are not owned by one person. Each individual brings themselves to the story. That is what makes a story

. . . *your* Imagination, experience, fears, hopes, dreams . . .'

'Film makes it so much better,' said Greaseball.

'I don't think it can,' said Shahr-Azad. 'It will be different, but not better than the story itself. If you capture the story in this way then it belongs to many people, the person who directs the actors, the person who chooses the actors, the actor themselves . . . You lose the essential . . . the quiddity.'

'Qu . . . quiddy?' Greaseball looked blank. 'Is that to do with money?'

'*Quiddity*,' repeated Shahr-Azad. 'The essential nature of it . . . the spirit of the story, that which makes the story unique. A story is a tale where the reader or the listener becomes involved. They bring their identity to the story.'

'Yes,' said Cy. 'When you're reading a story it is you that makes the picture in your head.'

Shahr-Azad smiled at Cy in agreement. 'Though they may be my stories in the telling, when I tell them, they are mine no longer. The story is yours.'

'You're prepared to sign off copyright?' said Greaseball.

'What is copyright?'

Greaseball stopped speaking. A shifty expression came across his face. 'You don't know what copyright is?' he asked casually.

'She might not know,' said a voice in his ear. 'But I do.'

Greaseball turned to face the Dream Master. 'Who *are* you?' he demanded.

The Dream Master looked him straight in the eye. 'Her agent.'

# Chapter 26

'**I** don't know what you were thinking of, telling Greaseball you were Shahr-Azad's agent,' said Cy.

It was the next day, Sunday afternoon, exactly one week since Cy had first begun his Arabian Nights adventure. Cy was waiting for his friends to come round so they could all go together to collect the runner-up prize they'd won and to give their support to Lauren and her friends who were due to perform later.

'I confess I was tempted by some of the offers Greaseball was talking about,' said the Dream

Master. 'Especially, when he mentioned merchandising. There's a lot of mileage in merchandising, you know.'

'They might have produced a Dream Master doll,' Cy said pointedly.

'That idea has a certain attraction,' mused the Dream Master.

'You're joking!'

'If it was a tasteful representation . . . ?'

'No,' said Cy firmly.

'Perhaps . . . mugs, pens, pencils?' the Dream Master said wistfully.

'. . . clothes, jewellery . . . skateboards,' continued Shahr-Azad with a sigh.

'Lampshades, toilet-roll holders,' Cy added

The Dream Master made a face.

'Exactly.' Cy looked at them both severely. 'Once *that* genie is out of its bottle, there is no going back.'

The little man looked at Cy. 'You *are* getting wiser, aren't you?'

'Notwithstanding . . .' Shahr-Azad began.

'What?' said Cy.

'It means she's going to give us an argument about why she wants to stay here,' said the Dream Master.

'I need some space,' said Shahr-Azad.

'You've *got* space,' said the Dream Master. 'An Arabian palace or six, for starters.'

'*Personal* space,' said Shahr-Azad.

The Dream Master and Cy exchanged glances.

'What do you mean?' the Dream Master asked her. '*Personal* space?'

Shahr-Azad put her hand to her temple. 'I need to tune into my inner self.'

The Dream Master looked bewildered. 'What's going on?'

'I'm carrying emotional baggage,' Shahr-Azad declared. 'And I'm hurting right now.'

'I think I know what it is,' said Cy.

'I've got issues to resolve,' said Shahr-Azad. 'I need to validate.'

'Why is she talking like this?' asked the Dream Master.

'She's been watching daytime TV,' said Cy.

'Oh no!' said the Dream Master. 'She's had her feminine consciousness raised by Operas.'

'Oprah,' Cy corrected him.

'Whichever,' said the Dream Master.

'Next thing she'll want is closure,' said Cy knowledgeably. 'It's quite important, I think. On these shows "closure" gets mentioned a lot.'

'Closure?' said the Dream Master. 'Closure! If she doesn't go back pronto and continue telling stories to the King, when she does she'll have closure all right.' The little man gave Cy a worried look. 'You do remember what happened to the King's previous wives? The ones who *didn't* tell stories?' The Dream Master made a sawing motion across his throat with the edge of his hand.

Cy shuddered.

'*That's* closure. Of the permanent kind.'

'Shahr-Azad,' said Cy, 'Greaseball offered you money. And it may be that he could supply it. He offered you fame. It is not his to give. And,' Cy went on with regret in his voice, 'it is not yours to take. You have to go back, Shahr-Azad. You have to ensure that your tales are written down, that they are recorded in some way for all those who come after you.'

'Princess,' continued the Dream Master, 'think of all the stories that will not be written, all the plays that will not be performed, the television programmes not made, the radio broadcasts lost, the films never screened. The children who will cry in the night with no story to comfort them. Consider the loss to the world without your stories to teach philosophy, learn logic, extend knowledge.'

'I do not need to return,' said Shahr-Azad. 'I have told my thousand tales.'

'Look.' Cy held out the book he had borrowed from the library. 'This is one copy of many, many, versions of your stories. There are millions of different editions in every part of the world, in every language that people speak.'

'I wanted to be famous here and now,' said Shahr-Azad sadly.

'But you are,' said Cy. 'When I looked you up on the Internet you registered fourteen thousand three hundred and nine hits!'

'O wonderful Princess,' said the Dream Master. 'History honours you. People of many lands respect the name of Shahr-Azad. The world owes you more than it can ever repay.'

'And,' said Cy, 'there is a reason that you must return. You told my Dream Master that I must not be denied my destiny. In the same way, you must keep faith with *your* destiny.'

'I do not understand,' said Shahr-Azad.

'You told me that you had told tales to the King for one thousand nights,' said Cy.

'Yes,' said Shahr-Azad. 'That is so.'

'So,' Cy went, 'the book is called the Tales of One Thousand *and One* Nights.'

Cy looked into the beautiful violet eyes of Princess Shahr-Azad. He kept his gaze and his voice steady. 'You must go back,' he told her. 'You must keep faith with your destiny. There is one more tale to tell.'

'I cannot do it,' said Shahr-Azad.

For the first time Cy saw a shadow within the eyes of the Princess.

'I have exhausted my store of tales,' she said. 'I have nothing left to give. There is no last story.'

'There must be *something* that took place in the last few days that will give you inspiration,' said Cy. 'Lots of stuff happened. The Dream Master disappeared. Everything went haywire at the magic show. The genie . . .'

'I don't know . . .' Shahr-Azad moved around picking up objects and putting them down. Her hand came to rest on the little enamel teapot from the doll's tea set. 'If I could find a character . . .' she said. 'And for that character I would need a name. A name that is plain, yet mysterious. A name that is magical. For this boy, and yes,' she glanced at Cy, 'the hero of this tale will be a boy. A boy,' she went on, 'who will travel far and have many wonderful adventures.'

Cy took his personal things from underneath his chest of drawers. He began to place them inside the secret drawer in the box that Shahr-Azad had decided to give him to keep his precious possessions safe.

Shahr-Azad watched as Cy put these objects away. One of her scarves, the matchbox with Arabian sand, the coin from Pompeii, his fossil stone, Grampa's war medal . . .

'Tell me again,' said Shahr-Azad, 'the name of the place where your honoured grandfather won his medal.'

'El Alamein,' said Cy.

'El Ala-Mein,' repeated Shahr-Azad. 'El Ala is such a noble name. And one that would sound very well within a story. Also I think that there should be a place for a genie in my new story, or a powerful djin as I would call him.' She rolled the words around her tongue. 'El Ala and the Djin.'

Cy took the piece of dreamsilk from the pocket of his trousers and placed it in the box. He touched the hidden spring. The lid closed on the secret drawer. Where did stories come from? he wondered. What threads drew together to weave a dream, or a tale of magic and Imagination? Many strands – a 'What If . . . ?', an 'And Then . . .', a 'Whatever Next . . . ?', a 'Just Supposing . . . ?'

'Just supposing . . . ?' said Shahr-Azad. She looked at the little metal teapot that contained the genie.

'Please, take it,' said Cy with relief. He gave the teapot a quick rub with his sleeve to clean it, and then handed it to her.

'So . . .' Shahr-Azad went on, 'What if . . . ? If, in this final story, we have a lamp . . . a genie . . . and a boy called . . .' Shahr-Azad pondered for a moment then her eyes brightened. 'I have it! This boy with the magic lamp. He will be known as Ala-Djin!'

'Ala-Djin,' Cy repeated the name aloud. 'Aladdin?' He glanced at the Dream Master. 'It's not possible . . .' Cy began, 'that just now, in my room in the twenty-first century, the story of Aladdin is being written?'

'There are stranger things . . .' the Dream Master murmured.

Shahr-Azad's eyes sparkled as she lifted her head to face Cy. 'I think I have it!' she said. 'Or at least part of it. I will return to Arabia to find Whatever Next?' She took the little enamel teapot and settled herself on her magic carpet.

'Peace be upon you, Shahr-Azad,' said Cy, and he pressed his palms together and bowed his head.

'May all the stories of the world be yours,' Shahr-Azad replied. 'We will meet again, I hope.'

The Dream Master nodded and his eyes were thoughtful as he spoke. 'That will be . . .' he said.

'Another Time.'